The Locket of
Moonstone

The Locket of
Moonstone

DADDALA VINEESHA CHOWDARY

PARTRIDGE
A Penguin Company

Partridge books may be ordered through booksellers or by contacting:

Partridge India
Penguin Books India Pvt.Ltd
11, Community Centre, Panchsheel Park, New Delhi 110017
India
www.partridgepublishing.com
Phone: 000.800.10062.62

To my beloved family

Chapter-1

"Your highness, a messenger has come to see you. Shall I send him inside?" asked a sentry waiting for the king's response.

Hearing him, a magnificent old man in royal robes turned to face the sentry, his skin glowing brightly as a contrast to his robe which was as dark as night with details in gold. His ornaments were sparkling with diamonds and other precious jewels unknown to many. He had blonde hair that reflected any light falling on it like a mirror. His facial expression was perfect for any king as he had many gestures involved in it. His only flaw was his age shown through the wrinkles covering his face. He was also holding a staff made by the finest craftsmen in the kingdom using the best quality of gold decorated with gems of different sizes. The tip of it had a resemblance of a snake with eyes of rubies shining bright red. As a whole he was a humble old king.

"May I know who has sent him at this time of the day?" questioned the King, with a gracious voice. It has to be admitted that he had a good hold of the listener's attention for this reason.

"Queen Aranga, sire." replied the sentry.

"Well then send him inside, Rastus." he ordered.

"Yes, sire."

Within a moment or two, Rastus, the sentry, left the room and headed towards the hallway. The hallway, through which he was passing, consisted of many paintings, depicting the major wars of the Morlan dynasty. Rastus was a trustful sentry which is why he knew about most of those paintings and other important secrets. He was working in that palace for about his life time concluding that he was just as old as the king. The hallway was a long one. He kept walking till he reached a small room. He looked around for any sign of the guards and when he was sure that the coast was clear, he reached his pocket and took out an old rusted key. It was Rastus's first time to peek into a room secretly, especially a one that was strictly prohibited. So he had to be careful and looked for any sign of guards. He had a fear that he wouldn't succeed and his fear did come true.

"Hello Rastus. May I know why you are rushing?" asked a sentry, who was just entering the hallway from the guest room which was quite opposite to the small room. He quickly put the key back into his pocket and turned to face the sentry.

"Oh! That is nothing Renato. I am just presently involved in an official matter which seems to be important." answered Rastus, trying to cover his fear. He started to sweat due to the tension.

"All right then. But . . ." before Renato could complete his sentence, Rastus left the conversation unfinished, but yet Renato seemed to encourage Rastus to continue his rush though he had an eerie feeling about it. He knew that Rastus was never afraid or tensed about anything but tonight he saw fear in his eyes. He wanted to ask him but he was no longer around.

Rastus huddled towards the gate of the castle. It was enormous, made up of solid iron and other bulky metal. The copper coating given to it shined brightly even in the dimly lit sky, as it was midnight. No wonder that a giant can fit into it without having to bend.

Near the gate there were two soldiers standing on the either sides of it who were half asleep. They were indeed drooling.

As Rastus reached the gate, he opened it with force. He looked around for the messenger, but found no one except for the guards who were about to fall. He got very annoyed by that sight.

"Wake up you idiots! This is not the time to sleep." shouted Rastus. He was frustrated due to the incomplete work done by him (though it was not good) and hence showed his anger on the guards trying to act normal.

The guards got up at once and looked around to face Rastus with an angry face.

"Where is the messenger?" asked a guard, astonished to see that he was missing.

"Are you gone crazy? You want me to search for him?" screamed Rastus.

"We are sorry, sir." said the guards who seemed to be coming to their senses lately.

"Is this the time to make amends?"

"No, sir." answered a guard.

"Then search for him!" said Rastus. He started to shiver due to fright about being caught and even the guards seemed to accompany him. It was midsummer, but yet the weather was cold. The guards were identical twins and seemed a little young for this job. They searched around for him but found no one, yet, they made their last attempt by running to the other side of the castle and found a boy aged thirteen, sitting on a rock nearby his horse. He was wearing a black cloak clung tightly to his neck. His face wasn't clearly visible as his dark hair fell upon his face.

"Hey! Why are you sitting here? You were supposed to be with the guards. Aren't you aware of it?" shouted Rastus.

The boy didn't respond to Rastus for a while. But hearing him shout forced the messenger to face the three men.

"Hello, I am Rastus. The King has accepted your arrival and he wants you in his chamber as you said that you have come here to bring in an important message." he said with a rather better voice. He preferred to talk politely than harshly as the messenger didn't respond to him at first.

The boy looked up. He had magnificent blue eyes that reflected a glow. Looking at those made the three men feel quite warm and comfortable though it was chilly out. He had pale white skin. His robe seemed costly for a messenger, and he was holding a long sword in his hands, which was made of bronze. It must have enabled him to kill his enemies from a distance.

"That's a nice sword." complimented Rastus, waiting for his response.

"Thank you." replied the boy at last.

Thunder storms started ravaging all around. The sky was enveloped in gray clouds. Rastus had quite a long experience about the weather psychology and hence guessed that it would rain

"Come on now, you don't want to get drenched in the rain, do you? The sky is quite wild enough and I suppose it can lead to a storm."

The boy in black robes got up from his so called chair and followed them. They rushed towards the castle to escape the rain, but it caught them.

They reached the castle in a minute and left the guards behind near the entrance. As they were walking through the hallway, the whirling sound of the rain died out. But the thunder bolt flashed once in a while reminding them about the wild rain. The sword held by the boy reflected the light falling on it. He looked so serene and calm, that made Rastus sometimes feel that he was no longer behind him. To ensure it, he turned back from time to time.

When they reached the King's chamber the boy saw an old man sitting on a throne. He looked much like a king, but he suspected him to be the King's father rather as he looked old. Well he was proven wrong as Rastus whispered to him that the old man was the King who yet rules their kingdom. The King got up from his throne as he saw the boy.

"Your highness, he is the messenger sent by Queen Aranga." said Rastus, pointing towards the boy.

The King walked towards the boy. He widened his eyes and tried to scrutinize him. The messenger bowed to show his respect and honor. Meanwhile Rastus sensed that the air was no longer fresh as it smelled of damp mud due to the rain.

"Rastus, give us a minute. I would like to have a private talk with him." ordered the King.

"Of course, sire."

Following the King's orders, Rastus left the two in silence. The sound made by his feet was the only noise in there. Just as the sentry left the room, the King witnessed a case in the boy's hands. He stared at the boy for a while just to ensure that he was no threat. The king had a strong feeling that he knew the boy as he looked familiar. Due to the fleeting looks by the king, the boy felt very annoying as he wasn't exposed to such situations. He took the scroll out from a case he was holding. The case could have rather been called a covering for the scroll as it was so thin and worn out. But yet the scroll looked attractive with its golden coat shining brightly. The king unrolled the scroll and found that it was written in Mora–their ancient language.

"Your name messenger?"

"Imas Hyde, sire." answered the boy, revealing his gentle voice to the king.

"Can you please read out the scroll Imas?" requested the King.

"Yes, sire."

The King was looking forth to hear the message written in the scroll expecting it to be a matter of concern.

"Your highness, before I read this scroll, there is a vital issue for you. But I am afraid that this news may cause you to fall into depression. "Imas interrupted for a while, staring at the King for any changes.

"And what is it?" asked the King.

"Queen Aranga is dead, sire." informed Imas.

Aranga and Cephas were grown as siblings since they were born. They were commonly known as the heirs of moonstone because they ascended the possession of it. When the king heard this from Imas, he was taken aback.

"Queen Aranga is dead?" repeated King Cephas.

His voice was barely heard as he was in grief. He was shocked to hear that news all of a sudden. He was rather perplexed by the situation and took some time to understand what was going on.

"When did she die?" inquired Cephas.

"Two days before, sire." answered Imas.

"How did she die?" asked Cephas, turning around to face his throne. He walked back to his throne and sat on it. Meanwhile Imas went near a window and stared at the stars completely covered by the gray clouds.

"She was murdered by Lord Rak, sire."

"What?"

"The last words she spoke were written in this scroll by her son that is Me." defined Imas with a voice that was rather depressed.

"Did he take over the Kingdom?"

"Yes, my lord."

"What are you left with then?" asked the king with a feeling of pity for the boy.

"My life and an oath, sir." replied Imas, trying to be sensible.

"Carry on." said Cephas who was about to cry.

"That night, it was raining heavily; we could rather relate it to a wild storm like this one. I and my mother stood there in the balcony watching the night sky dancing to the sound of the thunder, which once in a while stroke the ground. We were enjoying the nature's mystery talking along with a cup of hot chocolate. But all of a sudden our attention turned to a person of earthen skin tone, standing in the midst of the night. He was completely drenched in the rain and yet continued to stand there and stared at our castle. We wondered who he might be as he was there for quite a long time. We were annoyed by his stare. My mother, who always ensured my safety, ordered one of our guards to keep an eye on him. Following her order, he went to the stranger and inquired who he was. Before he completed his investigation, the stranger took out a sword and stabbed the guard brutally. We were astonished to see that scene as our kingdom was considered the best in protection, and yet he appears there entering our rigid defense. He was really fast and attacked many of our guards. The wisest of them ran for their lives because they knew that he was powerful and is none other than the evil sorcerer-Lord Rak himself. It was then that we came to know that he has developed a special power that enables him to change his physical form. He rushed towards us, killing each and every soul apart. We didn't know what to do and neither did we have the time to think. Our only chance to live was to escape, and if we had to escape one of us had to stay back in order to engage him, to buy some time. So, my mother told me to run away. Before I could escape, my mother requested me to give you a message. And like that she saved my life from him. She also gave me a sword, and here it is." said Imas handing over the sword in his hands, to the king.

"She also said that I have a reason to live and asked me to visit you for knowing it. May I know that reason sire?"

"Yes of course Imas. The time has come to turn over a new era; one that is peaceful without these stupid things going on. But before I say you, I want you to read aloud the scroll to me."

"All right my lord."

"Go on." ordered the king.

"Dear Cephas,

I am desperate to inform you that Lord Rak has his forces strong enough to conquer your kingdom, as well as the moonstone. I am afraid that once he gets the moonstone he shall have no regrets and will turn out to be a monopoly ruler. You do know that we don't want our ancestral efforts of keeping it safe to go in vain. It is no longer safe with us as we lack the ability to defend ourselves. It has to be inherited to our holders and they should be informed about the situation very clearly. You do know to whom it has to be inherited as their time has come. I very well know that you shall remain as guidance for them, as they prove to be children lately. Imas, my son is desperate to know the answer as nightmares have been hunting him. I hope he gets his answers to the endless questions filled with curiosity as well as sorrow. I am sure that my son is a magnificent ruler, who is capable of self-defending and can also keep up the responsibility given to him. I am warning you that Lord Rak has developed a charm that can change his form, so beware and don't trust anyone unless you are very familiar with that person. This is my last letter to you as I am going to be killed by him. Lord Rak's forces shall appear in your province during next three weeks. Beware. Do not worry about me, care for those who should be.

From
Queen Aranga."

"Seems as though the situation is very tough." said the king wiping off his tears. His facial expression clearly said that he was worried, though he was not supposed to.

"So what am I to do now sire?" asked Imas.

"You have a lot to do. But till then stay here as you don't have any other alternative, do you?"

"Thank you sire." replied Imas.

"You never knew our friendship bond. It was so strong. Even the mightiest of our enemies feared by us." said king Cephas and continued again. "It doesn't matter now. You look so pale; did you eat anything?"

"Yes, but not much sir." answered Imas hesitatingly.

"I will tell you about your need to be here, but before I would like you to have a good meal as you require strength. I have to say this to another person also; so, I decided to discuss this with both of you at a time. Is that okay?"

"Yes, but who is this other person my lord?" queried Imas.

"Saynna Manemoore, my daughter." informed Cephas.

They fell in silence for a while staring at each other not knowing what to do next.

"Can I go now sire?" probed Imas.

"Oh, yes. Why not? Rastus open the door and come in!" shouted the king.

Rastus opened the door and came inside. He walked towards the king.

"Yes, sir." responded Rastus.

"Will you please show Imas his way to the dining hall. Give him an upright meal. After he completes his supper, lead him to the guest room and take a good care of him. He is a vital person in our kingdom." ordered king Cephas.

"Sir, may I know who he is?" asked Rastus.

"He is the son of Queen Aranga; Imas Hyde. Now go on and don't waste time."

"Yes sir."

"Rastus wait!" interrupted the king.

"What is it sir?"

"Alert the soldiers."

"Yes sire, but may I know the reason." asked Rastus.

"Queen Aranga's kingdom has been attacked by Lord Rak and she was murdered brutally. She sent us a message before she died that his forces are strong. She warned us that he shall be here within the next three weeks. So I am ordering you to tighten the security. If you see anyone whom you feel eerie bring that person to me immediately. Is that clear?"

"Yes sir."

Rastus and Imas left the king alone in his chamber and headed towards the dining room.

"Why didn't you tell me before that you are a prince? I am sorry that I behaved a bit rudely with you." amended Rastus to Imas.

"I can understand your feelings. It's okay."

Chapter-2

"You see that painting over there-" Rastus paused to point to a small painting with a golden-brown frame pinned to a wall near a room which was locked with several chains. The door seemed as though it was never dusted since a millennia. It was indeed the one Rastus tried to peek into, but eventually failed due to Renato.

Imas felt a cold air stroke his spine when he observed the picture. He felt familiar with it though he didn't know what it was. The picture denoted a depiction of a young man fighting a giant smoke figure. The image was nearly blurred covered with dust making it hard for Imas to guess what it was all about. But no worries as Rastus stopped near it and started describing it, "-it is an ancient picture."

"What's so special about it?" Imas inquired staring at it.

"What is special about it?" he repeated looking astonished by his response and continued. "It is no ordinary picture, sir. It was drawn by a famous artist named Ragnarok Griefheart. There is a hidden legend behind this picture."

"And what is the legend?" he asked looking forth for a good one as he liked secrets, especially related to a legend.

"No one knows. That is why it is called a hidden legend. Well many believe that it was a prediction of a filthy war that is yet to come."

"WHAT? Did people in your kingdom predict wars centuries ago?"

"Not much but they tell that this unknown upcoming war is going to be a turning point in our world. They also gave it a name, the great war of Ragnarok."

"They indeed are crazy people! How come they believe such things?" Imas said, knocking the painting to test its strength. According to his calculations it was older than he expected and yet strong enough to prevent corroding for a few years.

"How old is it?" he asked, though he knew the answer.

"9999 years."

"You've got to be kidding! I expected it to be a few hundred years old." he said.

"There is a prophecy too related to this one. But it is only known to Ragnarok or his heir. It is believed that Ragnarok was murdered by a stranger for his prediction of this war. Many suspected that the man was lord Rak himself. He was young then. So if you are looking forth for discovering this prophecy, you better forget it because you will have to find out the heir, which many failed to do so."

"Is this matter confidential?" Imas questioned.

"Yes and no. This was a matter of concern a few thousand years ago. It is now forgotten by many of the people, like you. I expected you to know much more than I did."

Imas had a strange feeling about that picture. He was sure that he had never known about it, but it was tempting for him to go and find out the prophecy which many failed to.

When he was 9 years old he remembered asking his mother for something impossible that can be done by him for which she replied that he will know it in the future. He was expecting this to be the one he always dreamed of.

"By the way how did you know this?"

"Being the kings personal assistant does offer me with this facility. He discusses vital issues with me for any wise advice."

"Do you find that helpful?" he asked with a sickened look.

"Of course, you get to know each and every secret." he replied.

Imas's stomach rumbled with hunger. 'Can you find me a good appetite please? I hate this description stuff.' He thought as he always hated to listen to this kind of stuff.

"Your description is perfect, but can I come back after dinner? My stomach aches." He blurted out unknowingly.

"Yes. I am so foolish to keep you engaged in this matter when you are tired. Forgive me. Here, come this way." He directed Imas his way to the dining room. They travelled for 10 minutes or so and finally reached a long corridor.

"How long is it? I'm starving."

"Oh! I am sorry, we are almost there." Rastus replied. He stopped in front of a golden door and knocked upon it. After a while two maids opened the door. Imas went inside leaving Rastus behind. The aroma of the delicacies made him feel like paradise. He sat on a chair at the far end of the room and the maids ran up to his service at once. Chicken with rosemary was his all-time favorite food and hence ate a lot of it. When he was finally done he thanked the maids for their service. Even being a prince he did honor his minions.

Rastus suddenly appeared out of nowhere and apparently guided Imas to the guest room. They were passing through the same corridor but the distance was shorter than the previous one.

"Where are we going?" Imas questioned.

Rastus knitted his eyebrows which very well Imas understood, 'You'll see . . .'

"Are we going to the guest room or to the King's chamber?" he questioned, though he knew what Rastus meant.

"We are going to visit the princess."

"You mean Saynna Manemoore?"

"Yes." Rastus said indignantly.

By that Imas felt that Rastus was apparently troubled by something. He wanted to ask about it but felt that it had no good to with him. But Imas started to guess what the reason was in his thoughts. 'Must it be the matter with Lord Rak? Or is he disturbed by meeting me? Or . . . .' Before he made any more guesses Rastus asked, "What is the matter?"

"I . . . . was . . . just wandering within." He answered sheepishly and then turned away.

"We are almost there. But look, don't try to act smart before her. If you do so you shall suffer." He warned Imas which felt like a comment telling him that you are weaker than her. He wanted to protest that he never feared and said, "I am a prince, and prince suffering? I'll see."

They made their way to a garden. It had many flowers of different species and various colors giving the garden a glow. Roses were fully grown adding a beauty to that place. There was a fountain in between with birds near it tweeting with their lovely voice. The bushes were cut evenly. Insects were swirling around making soft noises pleasant to the ear. Just then a girl of 12 or 13 appeared out of a bush. She had beautiful dark hair with streaks of purple highlighting it. Her pale skin was similar to her father's. She even held a violin of brown color. There was a carving on it, but it was hard to make out for Imas as she stood far from him. Imas and Rastus moved a step forward to get close to her. He tried to scrutinize her for any instant information. The princess did not seem to notice them and started playing her violin. At first Imas was unable to hear the music. Then to his amazement, fire ravaged out of the violin. The music then slowly became audible. The sound was so refreshing that Imas felt all his grief sinking. He wondered how it was possible and was about to ask when Rastus said, "This is just a charm that throws you into extreme feelings. You forget about your surroundings and gradually fall in love with the music. You can break this charm only when you have the perfect mental ability or when someone is speaking to you. She does this to draw the attention of the birds. Are you listening to me?"

"Lucky birds . . ."

"Maintain your mental ability strong, sir . . . ."

Imas moved even further and fell on his knees at once. The princess yet didn't find their presence and continued. The music slowed down and the fire was slowly turning into ice. Within few seconds it had a thick layer of frost covering it. The music fastened and this time Imas fell into depression. He felt that his life was a big mess. Starting with his father's death to his mother's death lately everything seemed to him as a game played by someone waiting for him to go in ruins. Tears enrolled in his eyes stating that he was about to burst with grief. It was clear to Rastus that he was back into her trap. Hence he shouted, "Princess!"

The music stopped for once and she turned to face them. Her eyes glowed brightly. The frost covering her piano melted rapidly, but Imas was still in her trap and said, "Oh! Mother where are you?"

"Who is he?" She asked. Her gentle voice floated through Imas's mind like waves.

"He is Imas Hyde, the prince of Walor."

"Seems as though he hasn't come to his senses, wake him." she ordered.

"Imas!" he shouted.

"Yes . . . . Yes. What?" he asked.

"You were trapped in my violin charm . . ." she said and added, "Hello I am Saynna."

"That was simply amazing. By the way I am Imas. Imas Hyde, prince of Walor. How did you do that? The fire and then the frost . . . ."

"There is a spell on this violin. It was gifted to me by my mother before she died."

"I am sorry."

"It's all right."

"Princess . . ." Rastus cut their conversation reminding them that he was still present there, and continued, "Your father has ordered you to meet him at his chamber. He wants to discuss a vital issue with you two."

"What?" She replied frustratingly.

"I am sorry to disturb you but this is important." Rastus said.

"Fine, tell him that I will be there in five minutes. Imas will also join me, is that clear?"

"Yes, my lady."

"Stop honoring me!"

"Sorry princess."

Rastus left the duo and headed towards the king's chamber. Meanwhile she left her violin on a stone bench and faced Imas. Imas stared at the violin. The carving was very clear to him. It was the very snake resemblance that he saw on the staff of her father.

She felt uncomfortable with her post about being a princess and felt about sharing it with Imas and said, "I hate to be a princess. I want freedom . . . ."

"You hate dignity don't you?" He said trying to be smart though he knew he wasn't supposed to.

"Yes, I suppose it's the same with you. I wish my mother was here. What about your parents?"

"They are dead."

"Both? Then who took care of you so long?"

"My father died when I was three years old. I have very less memory about him, but my mother died two days ago and before she died she asked me to visit your kingdom for guidance I suppose. I was indeed shaken when you played the violin as it played a game with my emotions."

"I'm sorry. I didn't feel your presence then. All right, let's go." She said finally ending their conversation.

Imas suddenly remembered about the painting mentioned by Rastus and said, "Wait, I just wanted to ask you about a painting . . ."

"What painting?"

"Ragnarok's painting. The painting near a small abandoned room . . . ."

"We don't speak about it. By the way who told you?" She said with a perplexed expression.

"Rastus told me that I should have known much more about it, but you tell me that it is very confidential."

"How can he? I'll see to it and don't mention this to anyone especially my father."

"Why is it?"

"You will know when the time comes."

"What do you mean by it?"

Saynna gave him a stern look by which he eventually understood that if he would ask even a single question, Rastus's warning would come true.

"Would you stop questioning? Have you always behaved like this?"

Imas felt embraced and started protesting about it, "Stop it."

"Did you just say anything as I was wondering if I could use my violin . . . ?" Imas fell silent as he knew what would happen. They both left the room and then headed towards the King's chamber. They knocked on the door as they reached the chamber.

"Who is it?" The king questioned.

"Father, it's us."

Chapter-3

I mas was nervous as well as excited to know what the reason was. He was framing plenty of questions to ask the king like '*Why did lord Rak have to kill my mother?*' or '*Can I lead a normal life with you?*' or other questions related to some other stuff. In most cases children of his age lead a normal life but his life had many surprises till now and he did expect even more wicked disclosures.

They entered the king's chamber. Saynna was able to feel Imas's warm breath as they lunged forward towards her father. The king was seated on his throne waiting for them. There was complete silence till Saynna broke it as she said, "Father, you told that you wanted to meet us."

"Yes. Come. Please be seated."

Both of them settled on a cushion nearby. They shared a few looks and then stared at the king for any response.

"What do you know about your parents, Imas?"

"Not much about my father but quite a lot about my mother."

"Define your statement." Cephas ordered, staring at a small timepiece. Saynna got up from her cushion but seeing her father stare at her made her feel that it was better to be seated. She mostly hated her father because of his rules. She felt being a princess was useless. She looked at Imas who was getting ready for his description and wondered whether he would like to be a free bird.

"Mother was a nice woman whom everyone respected. She was really kind with anyone and always favored delicacies. She also . . ."

"I didn't mean by her daily routine. Tell me about any strange behavior."

"What do you mean by strange behavior, father?" Saynna interrupted.

"Saynna, wait for a while. I'll be coming to you." He said with a loud voice.

"Not much but she used to be dull during her last days. All day long she sat in her room and when anyone would go to visit her, she would simply regret them no matter who it is."

"Did she tell you anything about a new world?"

"No. Yes. I mean who would believe in a new world. She was insane at that time."

"Father, you called us to discuss about a new world that doesn't exist? Please don't ruin my time. I've got more things to do . . . ."

"Stop it!" Cephas shouted so loudly that it echoed throughout the room. He continued, "No. Aranga is not insane. Whatever she spoke, is the truth in reality. This is really important for you to know."

"Father you've got to be kidding. A new world, it's quite impossible."

"Enough. Please listen to me completely first and then ask any questions. I've got very less time. Lord Rak has been living for about ten thousand years and is known as the best sorcerer of dark magic. Long ago when Ragnarok predicted a war, a war related to Lord Rak, he got angry at him and killed him. News spread to everyone and fear filled their hearts. Ragnarok had a special power. He was able to see the future and that's how he knew it about the war. Before Lord Rak's invasion, Ragnarok filled his memories into a locket. These memories contained information about a prophecy related and some other important things that would help defeat Lord Rak. When lord Rak demanded him for that locket, Ragnarok killed himself as he knew that if he would live, Lord Rak would protest for the locket. If he would have regretted to hand over the locket, lord Rak would have tortured him brutally."

"But what happened to the locket? Where did he hide it?" Imas questioned who was listening so curiously all the time.

"He hid it before Lord Rak attacked. Actually he handed it to his minion, a farmer and ordered him to take it to the king then. The king then hid it safely in a secret place only known to him. The minion, who helped Ragnarok, continued to be a farmer. The king once tried to read his memories from the locket but was unable to do so. He tried his best to read but every time he tried, he got weaker and apparently died. It was then understood that only an heir of Ragnarok could read it."

"Father but what happened to lord Rak later?"

"Yes. Yes. Coming to that point, Lord Rak was quite clever and knew that it was useless to try as it sucks away all your strength. He knew that he wouldn't live so long until the heir appears so he met a witch, his mother and asked her to give the power of immortality. She agreed with him and from then on he lived as an immortal for all these years waiting for the heir. Being an immortal made him some kind of monster as he tortured people. He mostly lived in the north, but I wonder why he has come to south. And coming to the locket, it is presently with us. You are not supposed to tell his to anyone is that clear?"

"Yes."

"All right." Imas said resentfully. Imas was always incapable to keep any secret with him. But this time he had to try. They remained silent for a while trying to accept the reality which was quite hard for both of them.

"Any questions related to this?"

"Your description is flawless but what is the relation between a new world and the locket?" asked Saynna.

"As Ragnarok transformed his memories, some forces combined to form a portal. A great power unleashed from it and a new world formed coexisting with ours. The last part about the portal, it was found only a few years ago. When Imas was born, an explosion took place in a small room in his palace. When his father went to check over it, he found the portal. But the radiation set by it caused a slight change in your father. That change hunted your father like a disease for about three years and he eventually died."

"I never knew that my father died like that. So my mother lied to me telling that he went for a battle and never returned?" Imas asked who was astonished to know all these secrets at once.

"Yes because she didn't want another panic."

"Father, is there anything related to me?"

"Yes. The actual truth is that you are not my daughter and neither are you Aranga's son . . ."

"WHAT? Are you kidding?" They said at a time looking at each other.

"No. I am not kidding. When the original Imas's father found out about the portal, he felt it was better to transform Imas and Saynna into the other world to avoid any kind of threat. He made a few friends over there and convinced them to swap the kids. He also asked them not to say anything with the kids. At present they are leading your lives in the other world."

"So . . . . you say that we . . . are from the other world?" She struggled to get that out as she didn't yet recover from the shock. She was rather depressed to hear something like this. At the same time she was angry at him for not telling this to her before. Ever since she wanted to live a normal life, and now her dream was coming true. All the emotions within her have shaken badly. She didn't know what to do and her eyes, they told everything to Imas, her very feeling at that moment.

"We are sorry to play with your lives but we couldn't risk dooming the world. Imas and Saynna, I mean the original ones are to play an important role. They have to rule the kingdom after us. If they are killed, the kingdom would go into the hands of Lord Rak and the people's fate will be changed forever."

"I hate you!" said Saynna and got up. Without another word, she left the room and ran away. She left the violin on the cushion.

"Saynna wait . . . ." but before he could finish his sentence she was no more in the room. He looked at Imas but was no longer in a good position.

"Imas if you don't mind can you please cool her down and get here after a while when you're all at your best to listen because even wilder surprises await you. I suppose it is hard for you to understand the situation. And forgive us, please . . . ."

"I get it. Don't worry we'll be here within some time."

Cephas was pleased to know that at least Imas (duplicate) had forgiven him. He never meant to do this but they had no choice then. Imas slowly left the room.

Imas's hands were shaking vigorously. He was new to that place and he didn't know where to search for Saynna. Even if he found Saynna he was not sure if he could get her back as he himself was taken aback. His first search was probably the garden as he first met her there. He paused for a second and then tried to sink everything. When he felt a bit better he continued his way to the garden. His memory was quite sharp. That enabled him to remember his way to the garden.

As he reached the garden, he looked around and spotted Saynna at the far end of the garden. He was delighted that he found her without having to try a lot.

"Saynna, I'm glad I found you. You shouldn't have run away like that."

He moved a few steps forward and heard her crying. He thought Saynna as a brave girl but never imagined her to be so sensitive. He had known her for only a few minutes but yet they seemed to understand each other very well.

"Please go away. Leave me alone."

"I know how you're feeling but don't you think this isn't the time to cry? Everyone's life is at risk. We have to tolerate the truth no matter what it is because it is the reality and everyone accepts it. Please come with me, listen to the complete story and then respond." He said trying to soothe her but he wasn't applying that rule for himself. Saynna slowly wiped her tears off and faced Imas. Her eyes told him that she was unwilling to go with him.

"I'm only coming to know more, not just because you are trying to cool me down. Anyway who knows what the future hides from us?"

"Ragnarok did." He said trying to make her laugh. The trick did work and she laughed.

"Who are you?" she asked and tried to smile.

"I am Imas."

"No. I am asking who you actually are."

"Mph . . . Let's find out. Are you coming, duplicate?"

She knocked him from the side and laughed.

"Yes but only after you meet an important person. Are you up to it?"

"Is that person any friend of yours?"

"You'll see . . ."

"Fascinating . . . ."

She took him by the hand and led him through the garden from another exit. The plants behaved like a big life-size maze. For a while they seemed to forget everything that had happened a few minutes ago. All they seemed to matter at present was only about themselves. Mostly royal kids were never allowed to go out and have friends but when Saynna said about an important person he was interested. He wondered how she forgot so quickly about that matter and started laughing. He didn't seem to find that matter within himself too.

"Aren't we supposed to inform anyone?" Imas asked with a feeling as if it was the biggest problem at that time.

"Actually this is kind of a secret place. Only I know. Um . . . . Did you ever have any companion there?"

"No. I wasn't allowed to. But you do, don't you? You're lucky."

"No. Neither did I have any companion. This one was found by me recently when I was exploring this place. She's really cute."

"So, it's a girl?"

"Yes. Look, we're almost there."

They stopped in front of a small door. Imas mostly forgot his way though he was very sharp. All his beliefs were now on Saynna. She gave him another look and then took out a key from her pocket. It was a golden key. She held his hand tightly. She also took out a small black cloth from her other pocket.

"Before going in you will have to tie this to cover your eyes from seeing the surprise."

"Surprise?" he felt a bit suspicious when she said 'surprise'.

"I mean . . . my friend . . ."

"Why are you stammering?" He asked to clarify his suspicion.

"Um . . . . It has become a habit for me." She managed.

Something was going wrong with Saynna. But Imas had no other choice than to follow her as he had no record of the way. It was a complete mess. But he had to reassure himself believing that he had met her only for a while.

"Okay." It was all he could manage at that time. He swiftly turned and then she tied the cloth around his eyes. She pulled it so tightly that it hurt a lot for Imas.

"Ouch!"

"I'm sorry" she said.

As Imas was wondering who the person was, Saynna caught his hands tightly and from nowhere she started tying his hands with a rope.

"What are you doing?" he shouted not knowing what was happening.

Chapter-4

Knowing all the secrets on one hand was irritating for him. On the other hand he didn't even know what was going on. The only thing he knew was that Saynna had tied his hands. She had also blindfolded him and hence he was unable to see anything. He wondered why she was behaving like that. All he could manage was to run off from there, but how could he go. First defect—he doesn't know his way back; second defect—he was blindfolded. On top of all this he didn't know who Saynna (the one who tied him up) is.

"Surprise honey." She said with a voice unfamiliar to Imas. He was pretty sure that it wasn't Saynna's.

"Who are you?" It was all he could manage at that time.

"Me? I am Saynna. Saynna Manemoore." She said. Her voice sounded so wicked.

"Stop lying!" Imas shouted aloud.

"Stop shouting boy! No one can hear you. You very well remind me of your dad—the biggest fool I've ever met. What an idiot he was . . ."

"My dad's neither an idiot nor a fool! Indeed you are."

"How dare you speak that? Do you even know to whom you are talking? See . . . that's why I call you an idiot's son. Your father too behaved the same way when I first met him. And yes boy, maintain respect, if not I shall kill you the very moment regretting my master's order, no matter what it takes. Is that clear to you?"

Imas's brain lit up at the very movement when she mentioned something about her master. His only chance was to think quickly before she takes any other action. He had also known that the chances of him escaping were very bleak. But yet he had to give it a try. The only thing he needed at that time was some time. He didn't even have the slightest idea of being attacked and wasn't quite prepared with any weapon or ideas to escape. But before he could think of any ideas, she warned him, "If you are thinking to escape, no luck. The maze was an illusion. How good have I grown in it? All the credit goes to my master. Now come with me, as I said I have a surprise waiting for you."

She pushed forward which felt very rash to Imas being a prince. His brain was working at full speed but there was something missing in the puzzle, and it was Saynna. Where had she been? It yet stayed as a mystery to him. But something made Imas go with her. Maybe he wanted to know about the surprise though he knew he was in trouble. All the way long he had to focus on his way back to avoid the previous mistake done by him. He also had thoughts about the surprise. Imas mostly trembled on the rocks but luckily she didn't lose grip on him. He wished for any supernatural help though he knew it was impossible. She suddenly stopped him and that was when he guessed that they have reached their destiny. He heard some *clicks* and *claps* and guessed that the gate had a tough security system. After the sounds died she untied the cloth around his eyes. At first his vision was blurred but then he made out of the dizzying effect. But the black dots were still dancing in his eyes. He could make out an abandoned hut in front of him. He looked around and spotted a lake nearby. There was a boat too on the shore. Except for that there was a forest—the way they came from. So he expected to reach the castle by this route or an alternate-to travel by the water, but that was secondary as he didn't know where it would lead them. Meanwhile she was trying to open the door. That part seemed a bit weird for him as she didn't try to open it using a key but instead she took out a rock which was in blue with black spots. She passed the rock in through a small hole on the door. Then she knocked twice on the door. After all this process someone shows up.

"Who is it?" said a voice that was so dumb.

"7-Avilla. Open the door now."

"Yes my lady."

Imas was sure that only her physical appearance was alike to Saynna but she wasn't actually Saynna (even the duplicate one).). He thought how foolish he was to believe someone whom he had met only a few minutes ago. He wondered if all this was a ploy to kidnap him—Rastus; Cephas; Saynna; everything was an illusion created by this dumb lady, but he wasn't sure. Before he could think anymore a fat man opened the door. He had a plump nose and tiny eyes. His hands were mostly with scars. His dress was a complete mess with torn out shirt and a pant that seemed too tight for him. It ran up to his knees and he was barefoot.

Without any delay she pushed Imas inside. To his amazement Saynna was there tied up to a bench. She looked very weak and was unconscious. There was no light in there and on top of it, it was midnight. He wondered how he could escape in that utter darkness.

"Who are you? And why did you kidnap us?"

"Kidnap? I thought you were all my slaves. Lifetime slaves. No. no, I wish to kill you rather for what your parents have done. But my master, he wishes to use you, how stupid of him? And look Madmaw, dare you say this to the master."

"Who are you?" Imas asked for another time. This time he expected a perfect answer as he was really perplexed by the whole scene. By her previous words he expected her name to be Avilla, but not really sure.

"For your satisfaction, my name is Avilla." He was indeed correct about her name.

Saynna was in no mood to listen to them. She kept moaning. The hut was small but there was enough space for them. If he plans to run he was sure that the remaining would have to fall down due to less space and the furniture.

"Madmaw, Wake her!"

Madmaw ran to her and slapped her on the cheek to wake her.

"Break me free from the spell . . . ." she moaned and it became clear to him that she was in a spell that weakened her. Avilla turned her pockets out and took her wand. She chanted something that was too blurred to hear and then pointed it at Saynna. Red light glowed from it and later Saynna turned out to be perfect.

"Now listen to me, you will be evacuated from here within an hour. Arrangements are being made for your journey. Any signs of you moving even the slightest distance, mind that you are in trouble!" she warned and then tied him to the very bench beside Saynna. It was kind of an advantage for him as he could make some plans along with Saynna. The duplicate of duplicate Saynna—Avilla, hadn't yet changed her form back. She looked exactly like Saynna. Avilla and her minion left the room and locked the doors. Madmaw had a hard time fitting into the door. The sounds of their footsteps died out gradually indicating that they were far away from the hut. As soon as they left Imas turned to face Saynna and asked, "What happened? How come you are locked here? How did she change her form? And do you . . . ." he got interrupted by Saynna who was really confused by his questions.

"Stop! You are going way too fast. I'll explain everything once we get out of here. At present our only question is 'how to escape?'"

"Is there any window here?" Imas asked.

"If you are thinking to jump out of it, no use. I have already tried it and she caught me and then she put me under a spell and tied me to this bench. First think of a plan to cut ourselves free from this bench."

Imas fell silent and they kept thinking for a while until Imas spoke up with an idea.

"Are there weapons over here?"

"I don't know." She replied being doubtful.

"According to me this is some kind of a small secret shelter camp for her minions. So, there has to be a supply of weapons over here. Look around for any suspicious place. If you find so tell me."

"But how can I? We are tied to this bench."

"Use your leg."

She gave Imas a look which either meant—Are you gone insane? Or you've lost your senses or possibly both.

"Have you lost your senses?"

"Just listen! Slide your leg. When you touch something ironic, drag it."

"I'm not doing it." She said simply waving of his idea.

"Why are you regretting it?"

"There might be spiders over there and I'm afraid of them." She said with a frightened look.

"Then do you have any alternate?"

"No. But . . ." She fell silent on her own knowing that she had no other alternate.

"Please." Imas requested. Saynna had to confess her fear or she knew what would happen if not.

"All right, I will try my best." She said at last.

"Anyway, what would spiders do in such a small hut? On the count of three, slide your leg and look for anything, I will try to move the bench in your direction. That will make it easier for you."

"Okay." She replied trying not to sound like a fool.

"One, two, three!" he shouted and as a result they worked together.

Saynna stretched her leg and Imas pushed the bench to her side. She found nothing on her side.

"There isn't anything over here."

"Try again!"

This time she went even further and found something stopping her. It was like a sack.

"There something over here. It's like a . . . . satchel." She said trying to sound perfect though she wasn't sure what it was

"Drag it."

Without another word she dragged it and placed it before them.

"Now, only if we could see . . . ." Imas resented the idea without even completing his sentence.

"We can use the window." She said getting excited. She was actually pleased to find out that there weren't any spiders there.

"Nice idea! Why don't you open the window?"

"Fine!" She replied and got up to open the window but Imas pulled her down.

"Are you gone mad? I was just joking. If you open the window, they will spot us and then our chances of escaping would be nil."

Saynna found it considerate but couldn't help thinking about escaping.

"I'll open the bag and touch the things in it. If I find anything like a weapon, I'll let you know."

He let his hand inside the bag and felt the things quite ironic and suspected it to be weapons. They weren't really sharp to cut things but they had to give it a try. His luck seemed to show up after all these days. He was thankful to whoever kept those over there and then thought of playing a trick on her just to taunt her.

"There are some old books over here." He said trying to sound innocent.

"WHAT?" she whispered and grabbed the bag from him. She checked over it and found weapons. She got frustrated at him for playing a joke on her and kicked him on his leg.

"Ouch!"

"Is this the time to joke? Hurry and cut me free from this bench before anyone comes to check on us."

"Okay. Place your hands on the leg of the bench. Make sure your hands don't lie on the leg because I am going to strike on its leg."

Saynna followed as he told her to do.

"I am ready. On the count of three . . ."

"One"

"Two"

"Three"

Imas stroked it with a dagger that he found within the sack and with a thump! The rope broke. Saynna threw the rope side and got up stretching her legs.

"Nice one." She complimented relaxingly. She took the dagger from him and said, "Same plan. You ready?"

"Yes." He replied. He was actually tensed as he didn't know her skills properly and now let her cut the rope especially in utter darkness. He prayed for a better outcome.

"Don't worry, I will not mess it. Trust me."

"One"

"Two"

"Three"

Thud! For a second Imas was completely frozen but when he felt both his hands he was sure that she had done it.

"See . . ." She stopped suddenly when she heard footsteps closing. Imas got tensed and didn't know what to do. They were too late. Now what?

"Any alternative?" he questioned her.

"One, but it is foolish. I don't think it would work . . ."

"It's okay! We will have to do it."

Chapter-5

The tension grew among them. Their only chance was spoiled. Now all they had to do was to follow Saynna's idea though it sounded so stupid. They sat near the bench-their same old place and pretended to be tied up. Now the footsteps were even closer. Within a minute or two, the door was being opened. This time they came with some lanterns. Avilla was still in Saynna's form. As soon as she entered the room, she had a look on them. Everything was normal for her.

"Enjoyed your time in here?" she asked with a cruel smile. Saynna and Imas shared a few glances and then looked at her.

"First things first. I feel so awkward in this form. Too tiny and sensitive . . ."

"Shut up!" Saynna interrupted her unknowingly.

"Mind your manners girl! Madmaw cut her meal for today." She ordered and turned her cloak all around her chanting some spells. She turned thrice and then suddenly green smoke erupted from the ground below her. It slowly spread until the hut was completely under smoke. It was hard to see anything. Saynna and Imas as discussed followed their plan. They ran from the hut when they were sure that the hut was filled with smoke. They had to even ensure that no one was following them. When everything was clear to them they could make out the forest and also the lake but they ran for the boat though it was a secondary option.

When they were about ten yards away from the boat they turned back to see whether Avilla and Madmaw were in or out looking for them and found out that the smoke was clearing in the house. They immediately turned away from it knowing that they had very less time and ran for the boat.

"Where are the oars?" Saynna questioned, who seemed to find them missing even from that distance.

"What now?"

They were completely confused. They almost escaped from the witch and now everything goes in vain because of an old boat. They had only one other alternate apart from the boat or the forest and it was to swim through the cold waters.

"Are you thinking what I am thinking?" Saynna asked trying to read his mind.

"Let's go!" he said and they both jumped in at a time. They were just in time to avoid the wicked ones. Avilla and Madmaw ran to the forest coughing. They were still able to hear her voice from behind the boat.

"Why does it always happen like this and how did they escape? I tied them to the bench and . . . how did they manage to cut it off even in the utter darkness. There were no weapons in there, were they?" she shouted at herself.

Emails and Saynna failed they plan to swim as they couldn't hold their breath for long in the cold freezing water. As an alternate they hid behind the boat.

"Actually, I . . . ." Madmaw struggled to get something out but was afraid to.

"You . . . . What? She grinned.

"I am sorry for that but the fact is that I . . . . forgot my weapon bag in there . . ."

"WHAT? Such an idiot you are. Once the master hears this, he will kill you and me together."

"I didn't mean to do it . . . ."

"Shut up! Go and search for them at this instant." She shouted at him and they went off looking for Saynna and Imas in the forest.

"I think we are safe now." Saynna whispered to Imas who was just next her struggling for some air.

"Are you sure?" he asked softly.

"Yes." She replied.

Before Imas could say anything, she got up from their hiding place. No one was there.

"The coast is clear. Let's go before they come back."

Hearing her say that, Imas got up too. He looked around to check for his satisfaction. When they were about to leave something appeared out of the woods. A beast! What now? He didn't know what to do and neither did Saynna know. They couldn't think of any other plan as they were tired to do so. The beast roared aloud. It had a head with three eyes and no nose with a wide mouth along with several razor sharp teeth. Its gray fur looked deadly with blood stains. Saynna was sure that the beast, no matter what its name was had a good hearing capacity. They had only one choice and it was to run.

"What should we do now?" she asked softly to avoid the beast to hear them. They didn't take their eyes off the beast even for a second.

"Run!" he shouted and without wasting any time they ran into the water and swam as fast as they could, without even minding the freezing water. The beast too ran for them. It ran too fast for a normal human. When they saw the beast advancing towards them, the scene looked a bit different. It seemed as though the beast hated water. It ran on the bank along with them keeping a track of them.

"Why is it not swimming?" Saynna asked even while swimming.

"Maybe it is allergenic to water. Now just think of swimming and not about the beast's behavior."

They continued to swim. The current became stronger.

"The current flow is growing stronger!" she shouted on top of her voice.

To their bewilderment there was a waterfall in front of them. There fear grew even more. The situation was filled with many twists. A water fall? They doubted if they could even live alive. They had to make a terrible choice—either to go to the bank, surrender to the beast or to let fall off themselves along with the water. They did make their choice, but it was too late. The water pushed them off the fall and for a second they didn't know what was happening. *Clop!* They fell into the rigid water. Imas was about to drown when Saynna caught his hand and pulled him to the surface. He struggled for air. Saynna looked for a preferable shore and found a perfect one. To her left there were few huts and to her right there was a forest. The sound was too high.

Saynna swam to her left. Imas had to cling tight to her for support. They tried their best to reach the shore. As they reached the shore, the first thing they did was to ensure that there was no beast following them. They waited over there for a while to get some air and to relax. The place they rested was covered with a few bushes.

Roar! From far away they could hear noises of the beast. This time they were sure that it would get them.

"I think the beast is nearby. Shall we hide somewhere?" She asked.

"The huts would be a good choice. When it hears many voices it might get confused and may leave this place. Let's go quickly or it might catch a sight of us." He warned.

They ran to the nearest hut. It was the smallest in that place but yet they had no time to make choices. They knocked on the door and waited for anyone to open it but no answer. Their time was running out. This time they banged the door loudly.

"What is wrong with them to open the door?" she complained due to frustration.

The beast's roar became louder indicating that it was even closer. Luckily a boy opened the door just in time. He was just as old as Imas and Saynna.

"Who are you?" he questioned. He had a sweet voice.

They didn't answer to his question; rather they rushed inside without his permission.

"What is happening?" the boy said who was stunned by the situation.

"Just close the door!" they ordered together.

By listening to their command he didn't know what to do and stayed there like a statue. Imas had no other choice than to close the door himself. After he shut the door, he turned towards the boy. He was still shocked not knowing anything.

"We are sorry to disturb you." said Imas.

"Who are you?"

"I am Saynna Manemoore. Princess of Morlan and he is . . ." She turned towards Imas waiting for his introduction.

"Imas. Imas Hyde. Prince of Walor." He said trying to understand her.

"Prince and Princess in my little cottage?" the boy tried to clarify as it never occurs to happen—two royals in a poor man's hut.

"Due to uncertain reasons we have to stay here for a while. Please don't mind us and who are you?"

"I am Lathor Hodgson—a farmer." He said with curiosity.

"Where are your parents?" Saynna asked.

"They are dead. I make my living on my own. What about yours? Being a royal you must have security along with you, where are they?"

"Actually we were kidnapped by Lord Rak's minion and were thrown here. When we were about to escape we found a beast on our way. Trying to escape from him we had to swim the waters and then we had a great fall off the waterfall and as we tried to swim ashore the first hut we found was our choice to hide as the beast was too close. So, this is our story. Um . . . can we get some clothes? We are completely drenched." Saynna defined.

"I think I have some but I doubt if it would fit you. Maybe I can get you some good clothes from Erimar but only if I could get some money as I ran out of mine . . ."

"We will give you as much as you need but get us a pair of comfortable clothes as we meet travel for a few more days."

Saynna handed her golden bracelet to him. The next moment he was gone.

"What happened back there? How did you get kidnapped?" Imas asked ensuring that they had privacy.

"I think you know the story till I ran away. So, when I was in the garden, I was thinking about my mother. Suddenly out of nowhere she appeared. Actually the fact is that Avilla Manemoore is my mother or so called one."

"What? You said that she died. Now your mother is our enemy? How could she even torture you?" he asked with amazement.

"I lied to you. Long ago when I was small, your parents and my father opposed her for hating me. She knew that I wasn't the actual one. She started to torture me as I grew. That annoyed them and they banished her to the woods. From then on she was given shelter by Lord Rak. She was then trained to kill. For all these years of her grudge against me she wanted to kill us at the moment but had to follow Lord Rak's orders."

"She is gone insane!" he commented.

"Back to the concerned matter, when she appeared I had pity for her and went and hugged her and before I knew anything, she got me tied up and put me in that hut. She then chanted a charm and turned herself into me. You see she did exactly change her form like Lord Rak, but she faces a lot of trouble doing it. She just turned young and looked exactly like me. The fact is she can do it only in the presence of that person. She is a new learner so she faces blows up the place. Then she went back to get you. I tried to escape in the meanwhile but I didn't notice that Madmaw was there. He caught me and informed her. She then came back and put me on that spell and later you know what happened." She ended at last.

"Long one . . ." He said.

"What about yourself?" She cut in.

Imas then narrated his part of the story and just when he completed, someone knocked the door. They expected it to be Lathor and opened the door.

"Welcome." Saynna said.

"Here, take these Imas and you can change here. Um . . . Saynna I am sorry that I couldn't find one for you. Maybe you can visit Nerille. She lives at the far end of this valley."

"All right, but I couldn't just go there as I don't know her and we had a hard time trusting people. So . . ." she paused for a while waiting for his response.

"At present I am busy. I'm sorry. Nerille is my cousin so I am sure that you can trust her."

Saynna was about to leave when Imas stopped him.

"Be careful." He warned.

"You be careful." She replied and then turned away and left the room. She shut the door and looked around for a better sight this time. The Sun shone brightly and the sound of the water was refreshing and also reminded Saynna about the beast. She wondered where it might have gone.

The village was wonderful. She looked to the far end of the valley and spotted a hut. It was bigger than Lathor's. Without wasting any time she rushed. Her gown was still wet. Her hair was dried but was tangled. She needed a good comfortable dress without ornaments and a comb and hair band for her hair.

Suddenly a questioned popped into her head, *Where am I?*

Chapter-6

Saynna knocked on the door. Within a while an old woman opened the door. Saynna didn't expect Lathor's cousin to be a very old woman.

"Is your name Nerille?" she asked.

The woman didn't respond. Saynna asked for another time, "Are you named Nerille?"

"Sisiande?" she said at last but in some other language. She was unable to understand anything. It was sure to her that she needed a translator.

"Do you speak English?" Saynna asked though she knew that it was of no use.

"Nerille?" She asked Saynna. Hope returned to her.

"Yes, I am looking for Nerille."

The old woman pointed towards the other end of the valley.

"You mean she is not here."

She nodded her head. It was clear to Saynna that the woman could understand English.

"Thank you." She said and left that place.

She ran towards the other end. When she was about fifty yards away from it, she could spot some kind of a market set up there. Vendors were busy selling vegetables and sorcerers were looking for customers who needed spells and charms to help them.

As she reached the market, she looked around for anyone who could help her. Not knowing where she was, gave her a big trouble. For instance she walked through the crowd, everyone stared at her. That sight was maddening her a lot. She got her courage up and asked a witch nearby, "Do you know where Nerille is?

She looked up. Her eyes looked evil and her hair was a big mess. She had long nails painted black.

"Nerille is over there." She said pointing to a stall at the corner of the market. There were no customers near that stall. Saynna was about to leave when the witch caught her hand.

"Leave me!"

"Nice gold. Who are you?"

"I am the princess of Morla." She said and struggled to free her hand. The harder she tried the deeper her nails went into her skin. Blood stained their hands but the witch didn't leave her. She started crying with pain. No one else around seemed to bother her. It was just like a daily routine for them.

"What are you doing?" she asked. Tears rolled faster.

"We don't welcome Princesses. We put them in the prison rather if you are lucky or else you will be killed." She said with happiness, happiness for torturing a princess.

Saynna was shocked. The witch pressed her hand even more with her nails. Saynna felt foolish saying the witch about her profession.

"Nerille!" she cried aloud expecting Nerille to hear her. Though she didn't know Nerille she wanted help from her.

"Stop it! Said a voice behind her. Saynna was pleased that at least someone has spotted her having a deadly encounter with a killer. She turned back and saw a girl who was quite elder to her. She was wearing a normal pant and a shirt with full sleeves with boots. She was certain that it was Nerille as she looked similar to Lathor. She too had blonde hair with streaks of brown unlike him, but with brown eyes rather than black. She looked really beautiful altogether.

"Leave us! You are not needed any more." said the witch.

Nerille took her wand out and started chanting some magical words. When she was done, red smoke rose from under the witch's feet.

"Playing with a witch? You shall seek salvation!" she cursed and then in a speck of time she was no more.

Saynna was free to go. Her hands ached very badly and blood dripped all over her dress.

"You are hurt badly. Come with me, I will cure you." She said.

Saynna was glad to meet someone like that after all these incidents. Her age might have been around 17 or so. She wondered why the witch said that she was no more needed.

"Are you coming?"

"Oh yes." She replied and wiped her tears off her cheeks.

She followed Nerille to her stall.

"Are you Nerille?" Saynna asked though she knew the answer.

"Yes. And may I know why you have come to meet me?" she questioned with a polite voice.

"Lathor asked me to meet you for any clothes as we, I mean me and Imas my friend have landed here accidently and we are in a worst condition to travel. So can you find me a good pair of comfortable clothes . . . ?"

"Why not come with me."

They reached the stall. There were clothes and a few healing potions.

"So . . . you sell clothes?" Saynna enquired.

"Yes." She answered.

"How come there are no customers here?"

Nerille didn't reply to her question. Instead she took a healing potion and poured it onto her hands where she was hurt. She shouted for pain at first but then slowly the wound was getting healed. She could feel no pain at last. Saynna could understand that she was not ready to tell her the answer to her previously asked questioned and hence she left the question.

"You can pick anything you want. You need not pay for it."

"Thank you." She replied expressing her gratitude.

Saynna went around the stall. She picked a blue top with black decorations and a black pant like Nerille's. She had to admit that Nerille had a good dressing sense.

"Where can I change?"

"In there." She said aiming towards to a room inside the stall.

Saynna was changed and looked gorgeous but not as much as Nerille. She wanted one more thing too.

"Can I get a comb and a circlet too please?"

Nerille handed a black circlet to her as swell as a comb. When Saynna was completely done she knew that she had to pass those evil people once again. This was going to take Nerille along with her.

"Nerille, would you like to accompany me till Lathor's hut?"

"You afraid?" she asked. Nerille accepted to go with her.

The door was open. They went inside.

"Glad to meet you!" Saynna said and hugged Imas.

"What happened?"

"For a second I thought that I would never see you again." Saynna started crying. He tried to soothe her but she wouldn't listen. Lathor and Nerille stayed calm. When Imas was done settling her, Lathor broke in, "Imas meet Nerille Wellner, my cousin and Nerille meet Imas Hyde, prince of Walor."

"What are royals doing in a place like this?" Nerille asked.

"They are in some kind of trouble." Lathor answered for them.

"Where are we?" Saynna asked lately knowing that she was in a different place.

"You are in Icewilde." Lathor and Nerille replied together.

Saynna had a doubtful expression on her face and so did Imas. Being a princess and prince prohibited them from going anywhere except for their kingdom. So, they didn't know where Icewilde was. Lathor opened a trunk near him and took out a map.

"Here, this is a world map." He said handing it over to Imas Saynna.

They were shocked to see it. They were almost seven seas far from it. How were they going to make it till then by three weeks?

"We are really far from our homeland. How are we going to make it?"

Someone knocked the door before they could discuss any further. Nerille opened it for them. As she opened the door she realized that she shouldn't have done it. Before her stood a Beast that Imas and Saynna met a few hours ago.

"Aaaaaaaaaaaah!" They screamed together.

Chapter-7

All of a sudden they find a beast in their hut. Imas felt guilty for involving Lathor and Nerille into this, but what could he do then?

"I come in peace." said the beast.

They were shocked. A beast was talking to them! All of them shared a few looks, and then they turned to the beast.

"What . . . . Is . . . happening?"

"I am a secret messenger of King Cephas." The beast replied.

"I . . . I didn't know that . . ." Saynna stammered. They actually were out of words.

"Your father hid many things from you, but it is not to be concerned now. Your father has been kidnapped by Lord Rak. He asked me to give you this . . ." He paused handing them a small box, and then continued, "Why were you running away from me?"

Saynna and Imas doubted if he even knew about his appearance. At first when they were about to escape he came and scared the hell out of them and now he tells that he came in peace. He even got them into danger (falling from a great height). They were really angry at the beast. They wondered why he couldn't have said that while they were escaping. Everything would have been settled then.

"Look at yourself!" They said.

The beast, without even looking at himself replied, "I am so handsome. Are you jealous of me?"

Nerille laughed and Lathor too, accompanied her. Imas and Saynna giggled not trying to hurt his feelings but they burst out in laughter.

"This is not very friendly. No, not very friendly. Why are you all laughing? Am I looking a bit awkward? I think it is my hair. I haven't brushed it for a week or so. Can I borrow a comb?"

They laughed even more. Their stomachs were hurting and tears enrolled in their eyes.

"Um . . . . Nerille, do you have a double size comb? Our beast is need of it." Saynna was making fun of him.

"Normal size would do." The beast suggested.

"Don't you think of it . . . ?" Responded Lathor and continued, "Look at your size. Plus, it is our order not a request."

Hearing them say that the beast looked at himself. He was shocked. He didn't even recognize his appearance lately.

"You get it?" Imas said.

"I don't believe it!" he shouted and then roared.

"Please don't make such sounds. It would frighten the kids." Nerille whispered.

"And also the villagers." Saynna added.

He didn't seem to notice their comments as he was involved in looking at himself.

"That evil witch, I am going to kill her!" he screamed.

"By the way what are you called?" Lathor asked.

He roared loudly and everyone fell silent.

"This is not necessary at present. You have serious problems. Do you deal with it like this?"

They all tried to recap what he said at first and found out the actual problem. Saynna's dad was kidnapped and they didn't even know the truth of their life from the King as they were distracted. What are they supposed to do now?

"I think he is right." Nerille assumed.

They had nowhere to go. Lord Rak has taken their only guide. Now they are on their own.

"He just asked me to give you that secret box he hid inside the small room next to the painting of Griefheart." They were all wordless, especially Saynna and Imas.

"My work is now done, your majesties." He said and then ran away into the forest.

"That was a fast forward play." Commented Lathor but fell silent immediately when he saw the tension among them.

Nerille took the small box that the beast informed them about and gave it to Saynna. Saynna didn't feel like accepting it. She asked Nerille to open it. Nerille did as she was told to and opened the box. She found a letter and a locket. The locket had a big white stone in between and two snake's resemblance on its either sides. It looked pretty. But Nerille wondered why a king would send this at this time.

"Saynna, there is a locket and a letter in this. Do you have any idea about why your father would send such a thing when you are in trouble?"

"Did you just mention anything about a locket?" Imas asked trying to realize that it was the locket of moonstone.

"Yes, there is a locket in this with a white stone in between and two snakes on its either sides with ruby eyes. Do you know anything about it?"

"It is the locket of moonstone!" whispered Saynna.

"Locket of moonstone!" Imas shouted. Saynna and Nerille closed his mouth tightly.

"Don't shout. Anyone might hear us." Lathor advised.

"You are in the possession of the locket of moonstone!" Nerille said still perplexed.

"Actually we are all involved in this." Imas corrected trying to scrutinize the locket.

"What?" Nerille and Lathor said together.

"Yes, you heard him correct." Saynna replied.

Nerille had to make a choice—either to help them or to let them on their own. It was the same with Lathor too. They looked at each other and then nodded.

"All right, we will try to help you." Nerille said.

"Yes." Lathor added.

"Thank you."

Saynna had been yet taken back. She didn't know why so many incidents were taking place at once. Now they have to embark on a quest whatever it was.

"There is a letter too." Nerille reminded.

The three of them gathered around Nerille. She opened the letter and started reading it for the rest.

"Dear kids,

I am sorry to leave you on your own but try to understand the situation. You both know that you are not the actual ones. Here comes the actual twist. The actual Saynna and Imas are dead. So you have to take up their position."

"What does this mean?" Lathor interrupted for which all of them gave a stern look which meant '*Shut up!*'

Nerille continued, "Secure the locket of moonstone. I am embarking you on a quest to find out the heir of Griefheart and to defeat lord Rak. You know how it has to be done.

With extreme concern
King Cephas Manemoore."

As Nerille ended, all of them looked at the locket. Then Lathor and Nerille stared at Imas and Saynna for any plan.

"Can I get the map back?" Imas requested.

Lathor laid the map on a table and then waited for any orders. He gestured all of them to gather around the table and they did.

"Any plan?" Imas asked.

"We indeed expected you to have." Lathor countered.

"Okay so we have to make one now." He said swiftly.

He tried to observe the map. The only problem with him was that he was unable to understand the routes and places.

"Does anyone of you know what this all means?" he said with a disgusted look.

"I agree." Saynna added. It was indeed a major problem with the royals. They were never allowed to study anything more than their kingdom. They were told that a royal should always know about his kingdom on the first basis.

"How are you even going to make a plan with a map? We have to find the heir of Griefheart first. Where do we start?" Lathor accused.

"He has got a point" Nerille agreed.

"On top of this, why would my father give no clue?"

Everyone got into thinking. Where should they start searching for Griefheart's heir? How long did they have?

"Maybe he did give us a clue." Imas said processing his brain faster.

"What clue?" Saynna inquired.

"The King told us that Griefheart send the locket along with a farmer. As Griefheart had no family, I suspect that the farmer's family is still alive. Maybe they did know about how to read it as Ragnarok would have told that farmer. Now only if we could find out what the farmer's surname, we might be able to succeed." Imas defined.

"You are clever." All of them said together.

"Thank you." He replied gratefully.

Imas has been always really sharp with his hearing abilities. He was trained to solve mysteries and other problems. Now he has proven it to everyone.

"But how are we going to find out the farmer's surname?" asked Nerille.

"That part, I think we have to clear it. Before that we need a good sleep. We have been awake for a lot of time and we feel really drowsy and tired."

Nerille and Lathor tried to analyze the situation and felt to leave them for a while. They indeed looked at bad position. They gestured Saynna and Imas to lie down on a cushion.

"Is it all right?" probed Imas.

They nodded their heads and left the room. Saynna and Imas were all alone. Saynna collapsed on the cushion and within no time she was asleep. Lathor too tried to sleep on another cushion but wasn't able to do so. After a while or so he fell asleep.

He was experiencing a weird dream. He was in a prison standing along with Saynna's father.

"King Cephas Manemoore!" He screamed.

There was no reaction from him. Imas was confused. He didn't know why he was there, and neither did he know why the king was unable to hear him. He tried again, "Your highness it's me, Imas Hyde."

It was the same again, no reaction. He tried to analyze what was happening, just when Avilla entered. Her original form was clear to him now. She had two colorless eyes and black lips. She had long raven hair which was braided. She looked totally evil especially with her cold smile.

"Hello husband. It has been a long time since we have met. How are you feeling?" she asked and then laughed aloud.

"You are not my wife!" he said.

"From when?" she questioned and continued, "From when you banished me into the woods?"

"From when you started to torture my daughter." He added.

"Your duplicate daughter? What fun did I have to look at her die in that world? I tried to save her but it was too late. I will seek revenge for that."

"At that time, if they would have stayed here, they would have been killed even faster than we expected. But you, what kind of a human are you? You joined with the person who murdered your daughter."

"When I didn't have my daughter why should I live with you and your duplicate daughter? I dint like her and so I tortured her and for that you banished me. It was lord Rak then who gave shelter and trained me to kill you, but I give you mercy. I will not kill you, but my master will." She said.

"Shut up!" he said out of all his will.

He looked really tired and Imas suspected if she used the same old spell which she used on Saynna. Imas knew that he cannot respond so he went on listening.

"I have a surprise for you. Aranga Hyde is alive. We have put her in prison like you, but we tortured her much than you. We took her almost to death."

"You will experience the same, once we are out of this prison." He warned.

"Wake up!" said a voice and added, "You have slept for too long."

Chapter-8

He was dreaming so long which almost seemed like reality to him. His vision cleared and beside him they were waiting for him to wake up.

"Mother!" He shouted all of a sudden.

Everyone stared at him. He then realized that she was no more. But something inside him said that his dream was a vision of what was going on.

"What happened?" Lathor investigated.

Imas wanted to hide his dream from them as he didn't want to be a cause for a panic at that condition. He just smiled at them and then got up from the cushion and replied, "Nothing. I was just having dreams about my mother. A normal one, no need to panic."

Saynna doubted him as he knitted eyebrows meaning that he was worried about something. She knew that he was hiding something, but neither did Lathor nor Nerille seemed to care about it. Seeing them Saynna too left to care about him.

"So how long have I been sleeping?" queried Imas.

Not one answered his question. Lathor handed him a small timepiece from his pocket. It was afternoon.

"So is it the same day or the next day?" he asked.

"Of course it is the same day." Lathor answered.

"So I only slept for maybe two or three hours and you all tell that I have slept for longer?"

Without even listening to him the trio gathered around the table where the map was spread. Imas went there.

"Where do we start from?" Nerille probed.

They thought for a while but Imas was still thinking about his mother. Maybe he could sneak into her prison and release her as she had very less days. They might be able to help them. But if he was up to it, he should tell them about his dream. He had to make a choice in the plans. He observed the map closely and pointed to a place named Blackdell.

"You want us to start our search in Blackdell?" Nerille asked quite astonished by his selection.

"Why what's wrong with it?"

Nerille and Lathor stared at each other and then prepared to give them a clear-cut, "Actually it is the place where Lord Rak lives. He keeps his prisoners in a dungeon there. You could rather relate that place to hell."

He acted as if he was thinking. He was sure that they had to release her mother first. He at last decided to tell them about his dream.

"I lied to you." Imas said instead.

"Lied about what?" Nerille questioned.

"About his dream." Saynna answered instead of him.

"How do you know?" He asked with a shocked face.

"Anyway just say about your dream and a plan." Saynna ordered.

As told, he articulated them about his dream. They listened with curiosity as their story was facing a major problem. When he was done, they were all taken aback.

"So, you mean that our plan is to release your parents?" Nerille asked.

Imas nodded his head. Nerille seemed to think of a plan to go to Blackdell.

"How long is Blackdell and do you have any means of transport?" Saynna investigated.

"We might want to travel in a ship as it is an island. So you want to take the safest route or the shortest route?" Lathor answered.

"Define your statement." Saynna ordered. She behaved just like her father.

"The shortest one is filled with dangers like monsters and other stuff. It might take us two days and the safest one might take about five days or so. The decision is all yours." Nerille defined.

Imas had to make a choice. A choice that is wise enough. He was sure that he was the one making the decision. If by chance he turns out to be wrong, everyone would be at stake. A choice—the safest one or the short one. It turned out to be his first choice from when he was born. Previously his mother used to choose for him but now he is doing it for her. To save her he had to risk his life. Everyone seemed to depend on him, even the eldest of them—Nerille.

Did he need time or safety? Actually according to their position they needed both. But it was not possible. He wanted to ask them for any advice and he did, "What do you think?"

Hearing that everyone in Imas's position. They had to think tricky. Intelligence would lead them to success. Everything depended on the route they would take. Leaving her father in prison she was unable to go for the choice of safety. She looked at Nerille and Imas but they had no expression to reveal their feelings. Saynna at last made the choice and advised, "I would prefer for the safest route but when you take it according to the situation, I suggest that you better take the shortest route."

Imas and Saynna turned to Nerille and Lathor for their opinion as they can go no further without them. They turned out to be their guides. The only people they could believe in at that time.

"We think the same. Maybe you know about it. What about you Imas?"

Imas felt a bit more comfortable when they themselves told him that though the shortest one is dangerous, they have accepted to face it for him and Saynna.

"I do think as you and thank you for taking these risks for us. We would be really glad for having you with us." Imas looked at Lathor.

Lathor took a small piece of stick and drew a line on the map from Blackdell to Icewilde. He then whispered something to Nerille that wasn't quite audible for Saynna or Imas.

"Saynna, you go along with Nerille. You both would arrange for the boat and Imas and I will be hiring a captain for our ship as neither of us knows how to drive a ship. So is the plan acceptable with you both?"

"Yes." Imas replied. Saynna nodded her head.

"And one more thing . . ." added Lathor, "I and Imas will also try to get the supplies for our voyage. And I am warning you not to talk with anyone unless I or Nerille ask you to. People over here hate a royal, especially a prince or princess of the south."

Nerille gave Lathor a look which meant they have a good experience. Lathor ignored it and started to take his bag. He looked at Nerille and then she understood that she too had to pack a bag and should set off to accomplish her job given.

"Imas let's go and who would guard the Locket of moonstone by the way?" Lathor queried.

"Saynna and I can do it as our work might end faster."

Saying that the four set off to get the work done as fast as possible. Nerille guided Saynna the way as she didn't know that place quite well. They were mostly silent, but not completely. Saynna is an unstoppable express of talking. She would only be silent at times when she is kidnapped or when she is in trouble.

"Nerille how long did you say it would take?"

"By our luck if we don't get stopped by any pirates or monsters we might reach there within a day or two. If not it might take us three days."

They walked into a narrow alley beside them. The people were not out so Saynna didn't have to worry about her getting killed. The previous time it was so deadly that she felt that her hand would have torn apart.

All the huts were looking the same, except for their sizes which differed a bit. That didn't make all the difference. From Nerille's pocket she was able to see some kind of timepiece. It was a fancy one of silver. Saynna wasn't able to make out any details. She did admire fancy artworks and had a whole gallery of them in her palace but what use is it? It was all occupied by Lord Rak's minions. She wondered how many minions he might have had.

"Nerille, which kingdom are we in?"

"Kingdom?" she repeated and laughed.

"Why are you laughing?" she asked getting annoyed.

"You are on an island. Call it the largest group of islands. Give it a guess."

"You do know that I don't know much more than my kingdom." She replied.

"You are in Icewilde, an island belonging to Freyden. By this I get to know that a royal has been always weak in knowing which place they are in. You are indeed humorous."

They took another left turn and now the coastline was clearly visible. The sound of the waves was refreshing. Now she could spot some people here and there with their annoying faces. None of them had a single smile on their face. They looked like Lord Rak's minions, most probably like Madmaw.

"Nerille, why are people over here so unfriendly?" Saynna questioned.

"It is not really necessary for you to know. This place is somewhat like a crazy place, but not everyone is crazy. Some people like Lathor, Erimar, and you can count me on that list if you wish so. If you are really interested in knowing much about this place, you better know it on your own." She answered.

Saynna pictured how it would be if she was in this place for a week or more.

"You are really talkative. It is the first time I have met any invaders. You are so curious to know."

Saynna stayed silent. She tried her best to keep quiet. Nerille started to run all of a sudden. Saynna too followed her as fast as she could. She had to admit that Nerille was a good athlete but why did she run? That was strange. Traders were near the boats waiting for customers. Nerille stopped in front of a ship that was looking traditional. Saynna wondered why a person would choose a traditional one beside many modern ships. Near that boat there was no one. Nerille looked around but found no one. She was about to leave but it was the only one there (of her choice), so she had to wait.

"What's wrong Nerille? Why did you run suddenly? Any problem? And why are we standing here in front of an old boat? We could rather go for the one that is modern."

"Now stop it! Stay silent. Someone is following us. That is why I had to run. Now listen, you stay here and wait for anyone to come, and I will be looking at you from behind the trees. In that way we might stand a chance to know who is following us. Now do as I say and don't speak to anyone. Is that clear?"

Saynna nodded her head. There was a rock nearby and Saynna went and sat on it. Nerille slowly moved away from her and hid behind the trees. She waited there for and yet no one came. The plants near her were thorny and hence she felt really itchy. She bent down to have a better look at Saynna and suddenly someone patted her from the back. She got so nervous that she almost jumped out of the bushes but that person pulled her back without Saynna noticing.

Nerille got tensed and tried to free herself but to her amazement it was a boy of her age. She herself wondered why a person would like to talk to her especially a person in her village. He looked handsome with golden curly hair and his outfits were a bit odd. He had green eyes. He wore a cloak that had a snake resemblance.

"Who are you?" Nerille inquired.

The boy suddenly closed her mouth. He seemed to be friendly but Nerille was unable to believe whatever she saw.

"I am Kireb Mithun. I want to speak to you. Actually it is kind of important. I was waiting near your house for about 10 hours or so but I never found the perfect opportunity. So at last when we get the time to speak, listen to me first. I would like to have you introduced to me though I very well know you. But before that I myself would introduce to you. I live near you but you never noticed me. Actually fact to be spoken, you never noticed people anyone except for when anyone seeks you which is rare. I am a trader. That ship over there, where your friend is sitting is mine. So if you want it, I wish to make a deal with you. If you would like to be a friend of mine, you can get that ship and also a captain. So make your choice and expecting you not to shout loudly, I am taking my hand off." He said and removed his hand from her mouth. She gasped for breath and then stared at him.

"Look I don't know you, meaning that you are a stranger to me, and I don't talk to strangers. We would rather like to pay for it than to be a friend of you. How much does it cost?"

Hearing that, Kireb got disappointed. Saynna meanwhile was getting too bored. She picked a stick from the ground and was drawing something stupid in the sand.

"Madam the deal is off in that case." He responded.

Nerille got angry. They needed that very ship for their voyage but he was forcing her to be a friend of him. She had to accept it, at least for Saynna and Imas.

"Fine" she said and they shook hands.

"So when is your journey starting?" he questioned.

"We will meet you here when we are ready. Might be in a while or so. Just inform us where you live and we will come and consult you."

"I stay here all the time. So when you come, I can easily spot you."

Nerille turned away and started to leave but he caught her hand and said, "Thank You."

"Actually you forced me to."

She finally ran towards Saynna. Looking at Nerille, she too got up.

"What now? No one came here. Do you have any alternate?" Saynna asked.

"It is all settled. Now let's go and or we might be late to set off for our journey. We should be on the sea by sunset."

Chapter-9

Imas and Lathor were searching for any merchant. Imas didn't know why they had to search for a captain. Being a prince he never ought to do any work.

"Bad critique, huh? Lathor said.

"Sorry I didn't get you." Imas replied.

Lathor gestured Imas to turn back and seeing the scene he got shocked. An old man was behind them holding a Knife. He had long gray hair and beard that mostly covered his face. Imas wondered how Lathor was able to spot that man who was so silent. He doubted if he would kill him then there and yes he was correct. That man without wasting any time tried to stab Lathor. Lathor? Why was he stabbing Lathor? Any rivalry? Those were the questions revolving around Imas's head. Lathor too was quick enough to block him. He took a sword out of his nowhere and then the man too took out a sword attached to his robe which early looked like a pirate's. They were indeed having a sword fight. Looking at them, Imas backed away as he had no weapon and also had a fright of him being injured or even worse, getting killed.

Lathor took out a shield too from the air. Imas speculated how he did that. The fighting grew worse. That old man was so strong that he put the other hand on his back and fought with only with one hand. He was really quick that he caused a fatal injury on Lathor. His arm was bleeding. Nevertheless it was Imas the one who was caring about it rather than Lathor. They continued their fight. The sound made by the swords was disturbing for him.

Lathor made another swing with his sword and *click!* For a second Imas didn't know what was happening, but when he saw the disaster in front of him he didn't know what to do. An arm was lying on the ground. He didn't know whether it was Imas's or that man's.

"Lathor!" he shouted. Hearing him, both of them turned. As soon as the man turned, Lathor hit his head with his shield. His copper shaded shield has turned into a reddish one. Then did Imas realize that the chopped arm belonged to the old man. He somehow by direct or indirect means stopped the fight for once. That old man was about to faint and in a minute or two he did do so. He was lying on the ground. Lathor was looking at Imas. Lathor's expression was unclear. He was shocked, perplexed and grateful all at once.

"WH ...AA ... t ... ha ... ppene ... d?" Imas stammered.

Lathor looked down and tried to memorize all that happened. When he understood that he had injured their enemy (to be known), he was confused just like Imas.

"Thank you." Lathor responded.

"Don't mention it. By the way you fought really well but not as much as me. You need training." He replied bluffing.

Lathor shot him a look and then backed away from that site. He threw his equipment in the air and then patted the dust off his sleeve. He felt that it was waste to search for a captain and food especially in a lonely place. Within some time People would gather there and they might even be put under the prison. Sometimes they will even get tortured like cutting fingers and other worse things for being accused in a fight.

"We must not stay here for long. We shall simply tell them that we were attacked and apologize for not being successful. Now don't walk, rather start running as fast you can." Lathor ordered.

Imas ran with a great speed. Taking Lathor as an example, Imas too followed his orders though he was never used to do so.

"Why did he attack you?" Imas investigated.

Lathor ran even faster and Imas had to try his best to reach him. The sun was at its peak. He was tired, and eventually fell on his knees. Lathor continued to run not noticing Imas, until Imas shouted, "Lathor wait.

To get that out, he struggled for any leftover energy within him. Hearing Imas scream Lathor turned towards Imas but he was far away.

He got angry by looking at him getting tired very quickly. He ran back to Imas who was about to fall and caught him with his hand.

"Imas! What's wrong?" he cried.

Too late. Imas was in no situation to hear him. He just fainted. Lathor didn't know what to do. He thought for any idea and did find one. He took a wand from the air and then waved it around him and chanted,

> "*Tripante stiano grish yonn*
> *Merrito prefsenha killa stonn,*
> *Nyu freri getaritio jehen Crishkato*
> *Buttrure dren sackse analiato."*

After he completed, white smoke rose from underneath Imas. The white smoke took the figure of a feather. Lathor got up and continued his running. As he ran, the feather too followed him along with Imas atop it.

Lathor wondered why Imas fainted all of a sudden. His hut appeared in his vision. He expected Saynna and Imas to be back by then.

He reached the door and smote upon it. He pushed the door checking whether they were back or not. The door was open. Inside Saynna and Nerille were waiting for them. They were both seated.

Looking at them arrive, Nerille and Saynna ran towards them. Both of them were shocked to see Imas's condition. He was unconscious.

"What has happened Lathor?" Saynna asked.

Lathor was unable to tell them anything at that time. He himself was hurt and his arm was yet bleeding. Nerille got tensed to see him hurt. She tore a small piece of cloth from her scarf and tied it to his arm to stop the bleeding for a while.

"Did you run into some monster or any witch attack?" asked Saynna.

"Actually a pirate, or must have been a minion of Lord Rak. Anyway, I don't know what happened to Imas. He just fainted suddenly when we were trying to reach here. Nerille try any healing potions on him." he advised.

"Saynna, take Lathor inside and I will meanwhile cure him. There is some cotton in there and you can try to heal him if possible." Nerille said and then took her wand out from a pocket and started to prepare for a spell.

Saynna took Lathor inside and held him tight for support.

Nerille pointed the tip of her wand in Imas's direction. She then chanted,

> *"Frenato melano krisnat hyothi*
> *Tsiguni drevatri menn mennano,*
> *Xafiver anatier shricathe a laa vyothi*
> *Llok thahan ugilio cearo dtennano."*

Red smoke rose from beneath him, but eventually failed to work. She tried again. This time she chanted the words even louder. But yet there was no result. She tried again and again but no use.

She waved her wand at him and this time the feather was vanished. He slowly fell on the ground. Nerille picked him up and then somehow took him inside the cottage. Lathor and Saynna were inside. Lathor was looking better as his arm was no longer bleeding. He was drinking some water. To get their attention, Nerille said, "Saynna and Lathor, Imas is not healing."

"What dosage did you use?" asked Lathor.

"The highest one I've learnt. Do you have any idea why he fainted?"

Saynna looked at him. She tried to scrutinize him by having a closer look. Near his ear, she found a small insect. She picked it up.

"Nerille, Lathor, I think I found something."

Hearing that, they gathered around Saynna. Noticing that it was a tiny object, Lathor grabbed a magnifying glass from a table. He placed it upon the tiny insect (if you wish to call) and found a small tiny insect as they expected it to be. It looked like a spy insect.

"This must've been put under a spell to sting Imas." Nerille guessed.

"But who would've done it?" queried Lathor.

"Lathor, we have many unknown enemies in this world." Saynna replied.

Saynna quickly grabbed Nerille's wand from her hand and then pointed it at Imas and began chanting,

> *"Herla minto yuilp,*
> *Sisiande nidilp."*

This time blue smoke enveloped Imas and also the tiny insect and then the smoke rose up and formed a ball. That ball then went inside Imas. He at last took a breath and then slowly got up and faced the trio looking at him. He didn't know what was happening.

"Saynna how did you know that?" Nerille asked who was quite amazed by her work.

Saynna looked at Nerille's wand in her hand and then dropped the wand.

"I . . . I don't know. I just tried a small spell that I learnt from my father. I didn't whether it would work but I gave it a try and it did." She answered.

"What happened?" Imas asked.

They explained him whatever happened from when he fainted and they also narrated each other's story, except for Nerille. She hid her unexpected appointment with Kireb from them. Now all they had to do was to get ready for the voyage with whatever supplies they had though some are insufficient.

"So, Nerille has arranged for the ship as well as a crew. So, now all we do is to pack up. I will give you each a bag and then some clothes, as well as healing potions, in case we are in need of it. Imas and Saynna, I think you will also need some weapons and a wand I suppose. I will be back in a few minutes. Till then, Lathor take care of them." She said and then immediately left the room.

"Imas, help me find some food supplies for our voyage and Saynna . . ." He was interrupted by Saynna.

"I got it. I will have to look for some important things like a map, magnifying glass, compass, timepiece, binoculars and any other stuff."

He wondered how she knew what he was about to tell. They started their jobs. Saynna threw unnecessary things down. Lathor and Imas searched each and every cupboard or any box that they could find.

When they were done, Nerille was knocking the door. Saynna opened it and welcomed Nerille into the house. She was carrying a few bags suitable for travel and some clothes and flasks containing healing potions. Each one was labeled.

"So are you ready with your supplies?" she inquired.

They showed her some piles of materials required and Nerille very well understood that they had more than enough supplies. She threw each of them a bag and some clothes. They quickly packed everything. After 10 minutes, they were completely done.

They went out and Lathor locked the hut. They marched through the village avoiding unnecessary attention.

When they finally reached the shore, Nerille looked around for Kireb and there he was on the deck of his ship. As he spotted them, he waved his hand.

"So, Nerille, a 17 year old is our captain and crew?" all of them asked together.

Everyone stared at Nerille as if she had made the biggest mistake. Nerille just looked away.

"I thought that an old ship would serve us better."

They were still giving her the same angry looks. She tried to think of an explanation but she wasn't too quick enough for one. She thought of telling them whatever happened but before that Kireb covered it for her.

"Actually, today the ships are off. As you are in the utter need of it, I have accepted to drive you to the coast of Blackdell. One warning, I am not responsible for any dangers or fights. You should keep them off."

They shared a few looks and then faced him for any more explanations. Looking at their expression he quickly said, "Boys and Girls, I am proud to present you the one and only 'Wenytio'."

Chapter-10

An old ship was in front of them, ready to take off. It looked odd but who cared at that time. Lathor peeked on the side and found its name written in large, bold letters-

'Wenytio'

"Are you sure you are trained?" Lathor asked.

"Yes, I've been driving it for so long. If you are so doubtful about it, you may leave. Find someone else." He confirmed.

Nerille just looked away to avoid their fleeting looks. She stepped on the ladder and climbed on to the deck. Saynna looked at Imas and then at Lathor, at last she too followed Nerille.

"Are you both coming?" Saynna asked turning back.

"When you have made your decision what can we do, but to follow you." Imas said and then the three joined them.

The deck had a few broken areas. It had a few cabins in the middle and a small underground storage room. Saynna and Nerille explored the cabin to the very front while Imas and Lathor stayed on the deck taking a good view of their surroundings.

Saynna liked her cabin which was quite cozy with a round window on the wall near the door. There was a small bed too made of wood with a small cushion on it. Basic necessities were in a trunk underneath the bed.

"Nice room!" Saynna commented.

When Saynna looked at Nerille, she seemed to be worried about something. Her expression clearly said that she was hiding something. Saynna put a hand on her shoulder and then asked her, "Anything bothering you?"

Nerille's face turned blue. She managed a smile to cover her feelings but it didn't work. Saynna stared at her. Nerille tried to regret her looks, but eventually failed to.

"No, nothing." She said.

Seeing her cover her feelings, Saynna felt that Nerille didn't want to answer her questions and hence left her on her own.

"Let's go and check the other rooms." Nerille advised.

Hearing her say that Saynna very well understood that she wanted to forget about whatever it was. Nerille went out and within a while Saynna too followed her.

The air was so fresh. Cool breezes flew once in a while chilling out the hot temperature. Imas and Lathor were still standing out while Kireb was busy getting ready for their journey.

"So, Kireb is asking us where our first sop would be." Imas said.

Saynna without even thinking answered, "Blackdell."

Imas and Lathor stared at her as if she was gone mad.

"We need to stop in between, for at least once." Lathor said.

"For what purpose?" she replied blindly.

"For supplies as we were unable to find some."

Saynna thought for a while. If they would go through the heart of the ocean, they wouldn't stand a chance to stop in between. So Kireb is going to take them by the safest route! That would not work out for them. She plainly asked, "Are we going through the heart of the ocean or by the safest route?"

"We would take the shortest route by any means." Lathor answered.

Nerille seemed to catch Saynna's point of view. She too didn't know why they would have to stop in between when there would be no place to land.

"Where would you find a place in the heart of the ocean when there are no possible places?" she said.

Imas and Lathor seemed to understand what she meant. They too assumed that it wasn't possible. They tried to think of a place but there wasn't any. They looked for Kireb and found him near the helm.

"Kireb!" they shouted together.

He looked back at them and they gestured him to come back to them and he did so. He rubbed the dirt off his hands and then said, "We are about to leave. So, have you decided where to stop?"

"Actually, we wanted to talk to you about it. Are you taking us through the heart of the ocean or through the coast line?" Imas inquired.

Without even wasting time he answered, "The coastline for sure. Who would prefer to take the dangerous route?"

They stared at Nerille as if she has made a big mistake. Kireb smiled but seeing four serious faces, he stopped it. He couldn't understand why they were staring at Nerille.

"What's wrong with it?" Kireb asked.

"Look Kireb, we are in emergency. At any cost, we are going through the shortest one." Nerille described.

His face didn't seem to have any change and replied, "I cannot risk. I am sorry."

"Please, we have to reach there in two days. Our families are at stake." Saynna requested.

Kireb didn't seem to be convinced, but yet he replied, "I'll try my best. I thought that the coastline too had dangerous monsters, and now when you want to go through the heart of the ocean, I expect even more. My duty is only to get you there and I cannot give you the guarantee that you might be safe. So, as approved before, you must keep them off. Any damage will be paid by you. If you agree to all these terms and conditions, I shall take you by whatever route you decide." He described.

All of them nodded their heads without even considering the terms that he mentioned.

"All right, Blackdell it is then." He countered.

None of them had any idea about what was awaiting them in the waters. All they knew was to reach Blackdell, which can be considered the deadliest place for kids especially like them. It was indeed an unexpected journey cum mystery. Few nights ago, they were leading a very common life for their status but now, it has turned many directions. Saynna wasn't able to believe that she travelling in a ship driven by a kid two years elder to her. She even doubted if they would reach there in time. She stood there on the deck by the side of Imas and Nerille, and stared at the blue marine. It was so filled with small and big virgin fishes. The water was so clear and calm that gave a relief to her.

Imas was meanwhile trying to poke a fish with a stick which he found nearby. He aimed at a golden-brown fish. He stared at it for so long until he got concentration. Then at last he threw the stick. *Plop!* His aim was perfect. The stick penetrated through the fish, killing it. Blood filled the clear water.

"What are you doing?" asked Nerille who seemed to bother about him at last.

"Practicing my skills." He replied simply.

Saynna joined Nerille while Lathor was in his own world. They together stared at him.

"What? Is it some of sin? Well, I wasn't informed about it." He said.

The ship started to move. Lathor went straight to his cabin. The squabble between Nerille and Imas was not yet done but Imas forced her to forget about it. He too went to his cabin where he found Lathor already sleeping on a bed to his right. He looked around for any signs of dread and when he was sure that there were no threats he too collapsed on the other bed.

A white was clearing his thoughts revealing him to his dream world, which could partially be known as the reality going on at that time on the other side of the world.

His vision cleared up and to his amazement, in front of him stood Saynna, Lathor, and Nerille all tied up to a pole. Beneath them was fire crackling to burn them apart. The flames were high. There was no one else around. It was a dark room lit up with only one lamp—the fire. Sweat was rolling down their faces. He wondered what was happening to them. He began to analyze their situation. It was then that he came to know about a fact that most of dreams lately were based on reality happening at that instance, whereas this dream was showing his friends tied up to a pole in a different place. He also wondered why Kireb and he were not in that dream. Thinking of Kireb, he got tensed and doubted if he might have done something as he was their only unknown companion. Before he could realize what was happening, his dream faded of to another.

In this one, he saw himself along with his mother and father taking a warm cup of tea along with a few pieces of bread. This was one was quite stranger than the previous one. He very well knew from his childhood that his dad was no longer alive, but in this dream he was with him. Until now he barely remembered his father. In his dream his father looked almost like Imas except for the fact that his father had a beard and long hair. This dream stayed for not more than a few seconds. Suddenly there was a loud 'THUD!'

It took him a little time to realize that it was the actual reality. He turned to Lathor and found that he was still asleep. He was snoring though there was someone banging at their door. He stood on his feet, but h collapsed due to lack energy within him. He tried again to gain his stamina and this time he somehow stood up and managed to walk towards Lathor. His body felt heavy as he took each step.

'THUD! THUD!'

This time the noise was louder. Imas got frustrated. He wondered why someone would want to bang at his door at that time especially impatiently.

"Wait for a while!" he shouted loudly.

He stared at the door for response and when he was sure about the fact that the person has understood, he turned his attention to Lathor.

"Lathor!" he shouted shaking him by his shoulder. Lathor opened his eyes slowly and found Imas staring at him. Lathor's face was totally expression less as he didn't know what was happening. He wiped his eyes and then got up. He looked around and then he realized that he was in a ship. Lathor seemed as though he had had a deep sleep and looked perfectly fit for an adventure.

"What? Any monster in our province?" he asked in a humorous manner. He managed a smile but when he saw Imas's irritated face he stopped himself. Imas seemed to encourage this kind of management. Imas looked at him and pointed towards the door. Lathor too followed his finger pointing towards the door. He got stiff when he saw where he was pointing to. He replied quickly, "What! You want me to get out? What did I do? Was I snoring or something? If you want me to stop it, I shall do it at once. But why do you want to get rid of me? Oh, I got it. You want me to guard the ship? I am sorry. I didn't know it was my shift. I got it all framed. Now you can go and rest while I'll be doing by job. I hope you don't mind, but is it the fact that you want me to get out? If so can I know why?"

Lathor took a deep breath as he said all of that with a single breath without even waiting for Imas's response.

"I suppose you can understand signs." Imas said.

Lathor looked at the door and sighed. He looked back at Imas and then at the door. He kept on doing it until Imas paid attention to him. Instead of stopping him, Imas sat on a cushion next to him and put his hands on his face trying to cover his frustration.

"I got it. You hate me. Of course all the princes are the same. I knew it the very moment I met you and your friend. Something was suspicious, but I regretted the thought. For whom did I do that? For your sake, only because you were in trouble. But today you are throwing me out of this as you have everything needed. You indeed are a traitor. I hate you!" Lathor said and then started wailing.

"I never thought you could speak emotionally." Imas replied trying to be soft.

"Oh, yes of course. What did you think? Let me guess. You must have thought that my heart is a stone. I shall never forgive you for that. Go away! Oh pardon me. I will go away you traitor!" he replied.

Imas banged his head to a wall nearby. He didn't even respond to any of his questions. It was Lathor who mistook him for pointing towards the door. At last Imas took up all his energy and said, "I didn't mean it. I pointed to the door which meant that someone was knocking the door and of course I don't think it meant I was throwing you. Will you please open the door? And yes don't think I am a traitor."

"Oh." He replied.

"Oh" he said again.

Then he slowly walked to the door and then opened the door. He found Saynna and Nerille seated nearby waiting for them to open the door. Seeing the door open and a head pop out of it, Nerille and Saynna stood up and patted some dust off their back.

"What?" Lathor asked.

Chapter-11

Nerille and Saynna stared at him as though something
wrong had been done by him and Imas. They looked
troubled and frustrated. Their facial expression approved
that they were facing a worst condition. Lathor of course knew that
it meant about something else than the fact he and Imas took a longer
time to open the door. Seeing that kind of expression he gestured Imas
to come over.

"We have a serious situation." Saynna said.

Just when Lathor was about to ask what it was about, Imas was
standing by his side already gesturing the same thought. Even then he
looked sick.

"Imas you don't look good. Are you seasick?" Nerille asked.

"You caught me." Imas replied trying to forget about his dream and
yes the fact that he was travelling in a wild sea. It was Imas's first time
to travel through a waterway which indeed caused a fear within him.
He had so many wild thoughts going on within his head. He had a
fear of him drowning in the depths of the sea, or a monster attacking
their cruise, and engulfing it, or news telling them that they were lost,
or a storm. The list goes on and on. There was no limit for him and his
thoughts. Anyways he just wished he would reach Blackdell alive, no
matter what however they were injured.

"You might want to have a healing potion. Do I get for you?" Nerille asked gently.

"Yes, thank you." he replied.

Nerille left straight away to fetch a healing potion. When she was almost out of the sight, she turned back and gestured Saynna to tell them what happened.

"I got it." Saynna replied.

Nerille then walked away into her cabin.

"That is called understanding Lathor." Imas said.

"What?" Nerille asked.

"Ask him why it took us so long to open the door."

Lathor blushed but then told her whatever happened. Saynna burst out into laughter as soon as he completed his explanation.

"Seriously Lathor, you have to try to improve your understanding levels."

"Anyways Saynna you were telling us something serious."

"Our engine has stopped working. We need you to go and check the engine." She said.

"Why didn't you do it yourself?" Lathor asked.

Saynna and Imas stared at him as though he was a rare species found by their misfortune.

"Oh Lathor I must admit that you have a brain no larger than a berry. The problem is that it is underneath us, meaning that you have to go underwater."

"Why didn't Kireb do it?" Imas questioned.

Without even wasting anytime, Saynna answered, "Kireb says that he has to do some mechanical work on board. So he thought you both might help him."

Imas's face turned blue. He had a fear of drowning and Saynna tells him to go underwater for fixing something. He totally fell out of the blue. He didn't know how he would do it especially grouping along with a person who doesn't know how to understand sign language.

"Seriously Saynna you wouldn't want to kill me, do you?"

Just then Nerille came out of her cabin holding a tube filled with sea green smoke. It was closed with a cork.

"Now you can go." Saynna said who spotted Nerille.

Imas put his hands on his face trying not to show his fear. Nerille walked faster.

"I found it."

She pulled the cork out and poured the smoke-liquid on Imas who didn't what she was doing as he had his hands clasped tightly to his face. He didn't even feel the presence of the potion upon him.

"Work done." She whispered to Imas.

"Pardon me, but I didn't get you."

"You are now ready to go underwater as Saynna explained. I am done curing you of your seasickness."

"I dint feel it." Imas said looking at the smoke slowly evaporating off his shoulders.

"Advanced technology." Lathor answered instead of Nerille.

He felt better indeed than before. Confidence filled up his thoughts which very well helped him forget about the fact that he was at sea. No matter that he was still feeling a shiver within him, he was sure that the potion would cure it. It was his first time using any potion especially a healing potion from sea sickness. Well he himself forgot about it.

"You ready?" asked Saynna testing if the potion worked or not.

"Kind of." He answered sheepishly.

Nerille ran to the front most cabins without even telling them. Imas suspected it to be Kireb's cabin. Within a minute or two she returned with nothing but a scroll.

"Where did you go all of a sudden?" queried Lathor.

"Oh, I just confirmed Imas our plan." She replied.

She was indeed gasping for breath as she was rushing. She relaxed for a while and then she continued; "Now here's what we do, you and Lathor will go underwater and see if anything is stuck in the motor. If so you will try to pull it out. For your safety, try not to get too close to it as it might suck you both in. For that cause I and Saynna will tie a rope to each of your legs and when you feel you are in danger you pull the rope and so we drag you up. Is that clear?"

Imas and Lathor shared a few looks and then shifted their attention to Nerille expecting her to add something else.

"Okay." Lathor confirmed.

Saynna went to the supplies nearby and picked up two thick ropes and then joined the rest.

"You sure this would work out?" questioned Imas who sounded confident now.

Nerille nodded and took one rope from Saynna. The weather was quite windy and hence Imas suspected it to be evening.

"What time is it?" he asked to clarify.

"Evening for sure." Saynna replied.

"Where exactly are we?" Lathor asked.

"We have crossed about quarter distance. I suppose we are nearby White Lake. It is a deadly place for us to stop. It is said that the people who visited that island never returned. I very well don't know the reason why it is that way. Anyway now pay attention to your duty. Try your best to summon a sea god for our help." Nerille answered with a firm voice.

The phrase *summon a sea god* felt nice to Imas but he didn't know how to do it. He raised a confused expression which was understood by Nerille.

"You generally do it by offering ultimate devotion to him and for your convenience there are two sea gods and a sea goddess. They only help when it is most needed and to let them know that think of them for several times as you go underwater. And yes please don't think about all of them at once. Only have a single god or goddess in your mind as it shows spirituality to them."

"Nerille hold on, who are those gods and goddess?"

Nerille started laughing. Lathor too didn't know why her cousin was laughing all of a sudden. He too didn't know who those divines were.

"Look Imas, this is generally not known by anyone except for a few. Indeed . . ." before she could complete Imas interrupts her.

"Are you one of them?"

"Luckily, yes. Be thankful to me. First one is Dwiedus; second one is Wyd and the last goddess is Haies. All these were siblings but now their chain is broken. Hence pray only for one. The first one takes care of the water and it means only water. The second one takes care of the aquatic life. The third one takes care of the monsters within it. The choice is left with you both. Be wisest and not modest. Now we are rushing out of time. Let's hurry. Saynna tie one end of the rope to Imas's leg and tie the other end to that hook over there . . ." She said pointing to a hook that hung in a corner.

"And Lathor I would tie it for you and do the same as Saynna." She added.

She unrolled the rope and tied one end to Lathor's leg. She knotted it tightly that gave him a slight wrinkle on his leg. Saynna on the other hand tied it a bit loosely. Imas felt comfortable with it. They then tied the other end to the hook as thought before. When they were completely ready, Imas and Lathor took out their shirts and then shared a few glances.

"One . . . two . . . three!" Imas shouted.

At the count of three they jumped into the water. The water was quite chilly. No matter they might freeze. Lathor and Imas swam as fast as they could to the engine. They saw for anything stuck in it but found nothing. It was ironic and rusted. They swam to the other end for a clearer view. When they were sure that there was nothing they thought to swim back.

Something caught his attention. He remembered what Nerille had said and gestured the same thing to Lathor. He then closed his eyes and thought about whom to choose. Dwiedus or Wyd or Haies? Of course he didn't want to go for Haies as she wasn't much of help then. He thought about Dwiedus and felt him to be the right person then. Without wasting any time he thought about Dwiedus. Whatever Nerille had mentioned about Dwiedus popped into his head. Well she only mentioned about his duty. He thought about it for so long that he himself lost track of time. His breath was managed by Nerille portion and Lathor had managed a trick to stop his breath for longer.

Imas didn't know why but the dream he experienced a while ago gave him a migraine. It popped into his thoughts reminding him about it. He took a glance at Lathor and found that he was praying for someone seriously. He didn't know who it was but neither did he care. He tried his best not to get distracted. For another time the very old dream came back to his vision again. This time he almost lost his balance. He was slowly drowning stating that the healing potion's effect was fading. He suddenly felt someone grab him. Before he could get his attention to it, his vision gradually faded. He indeed fainted.

Chapter-12

"Nerille, why is it taking them so long?" asked Saynna.

"Well, they must've found something to deal with. If they are in trouble they themselves will give a signal as discussed." Nerille answered.

They stared at the water for so long until they had no hope left. Just then Kireb entered. He was smiling, which meant that they fixed the problem.

"They did it! Where are they?" queried Kireb.

Nerille pointed to the water. Kireb went and peeked into the water. He wasn't able to see anything as it was getting darker and the weather showed signs of a tempest. Just then Kireb observed the rope with Nerille being pulled.

"Look! I think they are signaling you. I just saw a pull of the rope. Quickly drag them up!" he ordered.

Nerille and Saynna started pulling both the ropes. Nerille felt not much stress whereas Saynna wasn't able to hold the weight. She felt something pulling off.

"Kireb, can you please help me?" She requested him though it was an emergency.

Kireb ran to her at once and helped her pull Imas. Meanwhile Nerille was doing her best. Lathor came into appearance underneath the surface, but there was no sign of Imas. Lathor at last came to the surface and gasped for breath. Nerille helped him onboard and then gave him a towel. He was literally shivering due to cold.

Saynna and Kireb suddenly felt a drop of the weight. They wondered why there was a loss of weight all of a sudden. Tension grew among them. After a few seconds or so they were able to see the end of the rope.

"Imas!" Saynna screamed at once.

She started crying. Kireb dragged the rope up and wondered what might have happened to him. Saynna was totally perplexed. Hearing her cry, Nerille left about Lathor and ran to Saynna not knowing why she was crying. Lathor tried to tell something but his voice didn't come out. He needed to relax for a minute or so.

"What's wrong Saynna?" she asked not knowing that the rope was cut off by someone or something stating that he was in danger.

Saynna didn't answer being busy in controlling her emotions. Her face turned as red as a cherry.

"Saynna talk to me. Where's Imas by the way" she questioned.

"He's missing." Kireb answered instead of Saynna.

Nerille didn't know what to do. She too was in a state of shock. She rested her hand on Saynna's shoulder trying to soothe her.

"I think we were late. In between we felt a drop of weight and I guess that was the moment when Imas dropped out or something. I suppose Lathor must've witnessed something while being pulled up. Ask him." Kireb said.

Saynna ran to Lathor at once and said, "Lathor . . . do you know anything . . . about . . . Imas?"

Lathor nodded and cleared his throat.

"When we went there to check as you told us to, we found nothing over there. Just then Imas signaled me to pray for any sea god as Nerille mentioned. When we were on it, I suddenly saw a huge figure emerge out of nowhere. I pulled the rope twice as you told me to. But I don't know why he didn't do as told. All of a sudden you were pulling me up but dis luck for Imas. The monster got him and yes I observed that he fainted too. Now I don't know anything except for that. I'm sorry we failed to do anything." Lathor described.

"Failed too? You corrected the error in the system. You did it correct. I am very thankful to you and at the same time I am very sorry about Imas. I very well warned you about monsters if we would travel through the heart of the ocean. Well it was your choice. Now what do we do?" Kireb asked.

Saynna tried to stop crying but whatever happened to him was yet a mystery to her and others. She didn't know why Kireb was so cool without much tension. Their next move was to search for him. She felt that they should have expected something like this or even worse and should've prepared for it. She felt it was indeed her fault, but thinking about it was no use then.

The weather was growing wilder. No doubt it would knock their boat off. All of them paid attention to it though they were involved in some other serious issue.

"Emergency! We have to stop somewhere until the storm subsides or else no doubt we might all meet the same fate of Imas. We shall search for him later. At present we will stop at a nearby island. No more discussions on this matter." Kireb said.

Immediately he ran to the front. Saynna felt sad for him but Kireb was right at that point. At the same time she felt he wasn't caring about Imas. Nerille lifted Saynna up and took to their cabin.

Lathor was left alone on deck. He guided himself to the cabin. A few minutes ago, he was there along with emails and now Imas was absent. His room was filled with Imas's essence reminding him Imas all the time. He sat near the window and stared at the wild waves. It was the start of the tempest. He closed his eyes and let away all those thoughts out of his mind for relief.

Meanwhile Saynna too sat near the window. Her heart was feeling a pain. A pain so heavy and deep. Nerille sat beside her and took Saynna's palm into her palm. She squeezed her hand for giving Saynna confidence.

"Do you want to know about a story of a young girl who lost her loved ones?" Nerille asked.

Saynna didn't respond, but Nerille continued.

"Once upon a time there lived a girl in a beautiful village. She was about your age then. She had a lovely family consisting of her mother, father, brother, uncle, aunt, cousin and so on. Their family was highly respected in the community. Every day was a fresh start for many new things to learn. Things were good going then until a landlord visits them. You can call that landlord as a destroyer or for accuracy you can call him Lord Rak. He entered into their lives for something not known to any. He killed everyone in that family. Before that, her family saved the girl and her cousin from him. They hid them under a bed. They tried to save her brother too but he was caught in the act. After a while she came out and found everyone dead. Blood was everywhere. She and her cousin managed to find a living later, but it was hard for them to control their emotions. They worked hard to earn a living and took up their parent's occupation at a very young age. No one helped her out then. The villagers who respected them started to dislike them. Whenever they would spot the girl and her cousin, they hid or either showed hatred to them. Except for two or three people no one helped them out. And out of those two people one of them was an old woman who at least had minimum belief in them and the second one was her son. It was a hard time for her to forget about them but she had to try her best. Her cousin was so young then, almost eight or ten. If you go deep into her story she lived a life of terror after her beloved one's death. And Saynna if you ever want to know more about that girl, you are free to ask."

Saynna listened to her but not with much attention. She still was thinking about Imas. Yet Nerille continued, "After a few years from then two kids show up at once. They could be termed as the first ones to meet them after that tragedy. From this you must understand one thing that whatever happens to your beloved ones, you must not go to emotional. Have trust and enough confidence that they will return sooner than you think. Even now if you wish to continue the way you are, I cannot help you. This is the only stage that I can help you."

Saynna turned to face Nerille. She wiped her tears and then lied on her. Nerille patted her.

"Nerille, it was your story, wasn't it?"

"Good guess. Indeed it is. Those were indeed bad days. Anyway it is a long time that I forgot about it. I promise you we would return back to search for him. Indeed he is the only one who knows about the complete plan. You are a lot attached with him, aren't you?" Nerille asked straightforwardly.

Saynna raised her head and stared at the blue water for a while and then she said, "I don't know."

"You'll know sooner or later." She replied.

Thud! Thud!

Someone was knocking the door for sure. Saynna wanted it to be Imas. But she couldn't expect it. He was no longer with them. All she hoped was that he was safe and would return shortly though the probability was low. Saynna was about to get up but Nerille interrupted her.

"I'll open it for you."

Hearing that she settled into her thoughts for another time. Nerille opened the door and saw that Kireb was waiting for them with news.

"We are about to land. But I'm afraid we are stopping at White Lake. I'm warning you for another time, be careful. Never go alone. Stay in groups so that we can avoid danger. These are very important precautions and please follow them. We will be camping near the coast but not exactly near it as we can expect for high tidal waves. Get your things packed up. Pack only the essentials and make sure your luggage is light, including weapons. Now hurry, we have only a few minutes before the tempest. Get some lanterns for sure as it is very dark. Now go for it."

He gave a big description that wasn't quite understood by Nerille. He then left the room and went to Lathor's cabin.

"Saynna I suppose you heard him. So go on as told."

They packed up a few things as told and went up to the deck. Lathor was already there. Saynna somehow tried to control her emotions.

"Nerille could you promise me on one thing?"

"What is it?" Nerille asked.

"Don't leave me alone. Stay with me. Please." She requested.

"I will of course stay with you. No matter whatever happens I will not leave you. Indeed you are my responsibility."

They walked up to Lathor and stood beside him. He too was depressed and stood there silent.

"It's starting." Lathor said.

"What is?" Saynna asked.

Before he could answer Nerille ran to his side and pinched him by the side. It was kind of a warning for him. Saynna wasn't able to understand anything.

"The days of the dark have started." He added without even considering Nerille's warning.

"Lathor I think we are about to land. After landing I would like to meet you. We have something to discuss." Nerille whispered to Luther.

Nerille was correct about the landing part. The island was just ten yards away from them. It was having a thick coat of forest even from the beginning. The trees were so tall and bushy that covered the sky. Within a while the ship came to a complete stop.

"Welcome to White Lake. The place that you would never want to see is of course White Lake." Kireb said.

"Kireb, stop kidding." Nerille said.

"Do you think it is safe to camp over here?" Saynna asked.

Kireb looked at her and then smiled. She didn't know he was smiling at her all at once.

"Any other choice?" he replied simply.

"Anyway, Nerille can I ask you why people who visited this place never return?" Saynna asked.

"You'll know." She answered.

Chapter-13

They had to find a comfortable place to rest and went on searching for it. It was raining heavily; hence they had to rush all the way into the forest. They knew that they were in some kind of danger. They had to be prepared from all sides.

"Get your weapons prepared. Nerille and Lathor take the front, and Saynna and I will be guarding from the back. We shall not take any risks. Now maintain complete silence and please walk slowly." Kireb commanded.

They were about to enter the forest. The weather was so cold with hail stones too adding up with the rain. Nerille slowly advanced. Lathor was just behind her and looked a lot nervous. He was also shivering due to the rain.

"How far do we have to go?" Nerille asked.

"Shhhhh!"

"Oh sorry, answer me." She whispered.

"Until you find a clear place. Now go on." He said.

She took a few steps and then stopped. Around and asked them to maintain silence for a while. They did so as she said. After a few seconds Kireb asked her, "What's wrong?"

"I think there is someone or something around here. Anyway I think it was just my imagination. Let's go on."

They continued to move on. They kept walking for more than thirty minutes and finally stopped.

"I can't walk anymore." Saynna said.

She went and sat on a nearby rock and asked Nerille for some water.

"Kireb you take care of Saynna and Lathor. I'll just explore the perimeter for any chance of shelter." Nerille said and then started to leave them.

"Wait!" Saynna called out.

"What is it?" Nerille asked.

"You promised me."

"Oh Saynna it is just for a few minutes."

"But please." Saynna requested. At that instant she was indeed behaving like a small kid.

"I'll go instead." Kireb volunteered.

"Thank you." she replied and then sat beside Saynna.

Lathor too sat beside Saynna. Kireb left the premises and went on looking for shelter. His footsteps were not at all audible. It was for sure that he was good at survival guidance. After a while he returned smiling.

"I found a cave nearby."

All of them were delighted. The hail stones and rain had died out just when they were about to get up. By all means it made no big difference as the trees stooped the rainfall.

They all stood up and rushed the way Kireb went. They stayed away from most of the tall grass as they had a fright of poisonous insects. After taking a few steps, they were able to see a large cave in front of them. It looked old. The walls of it were dry and clean as though it was built just a moment ago. That sight was indeed astonishing. It looked magnificent.

"Amazing . . ." Saynna said.

"Splendid!" Lathor added.

"Let's go in now." Nerille suggested.

"Wait! We need a lantern. Who brought it?" asked Kireb.

"I" They said all together.

"Good. Can anyone of you lend me one?"

"Here." Nerille said handing it over to Kireb.

They went to the entrance and then stopped in front of it.

"You go first." Kireb said.

"No you go first." Nerille said.

"No you go. I'll be at the back like before."

"No you go. This time I'll take up the back." Saynna back answered.

"Look I am pretty good at guarding, the back especially. So please leave it to me and this is a request. Please . . ."

"Kireb that is what I am trying to tell you. I don't think I can lead you all. Even I am requesting you, please."

Saynna and Lathor followed the looks of both of them. They were arguing like kids. Saynna took up the courage and said, "I'll go first."

Nerille looked at her and felt ashamed of being a coward.

"No, it's okay. I'll go." Nerille said at last compromising.

"Good then." Lathor said trying to end their conversation.

Nerille took a deep breath and went on. She didn't know why Kireb was being like that. She could see nothing in the cave except for their way. It was empty. She went on and on. Suddenly she found something interesting in front of her.

"Mind blowing." She commented on that scene.

The rest behind her didn't know what she was telling about. They were perplexed why she stopped.

"What is the matter Nerille?" asked Saynna who was standing just behind her.

Without even responding to her, Nerille went on. Later she did get to know what Nerille was talking about. It was splendid indeed. A doorway to a mysterious place stood in front of them. It was short but no matter they could fit by bending. Inside was a whole new world. There was a throne far away but no one was seated on it. The throne was just like her father's except for the act that it was ten times larger than it. It was made of silver and not gold which was very rare. There was the same old snake resemblance on it. She didn't what it meant and was curious to know about it. The throne was so far away that it looked small. The ceiling was clear cut in a wavy shape. It was also blue in color. The floor was white with marble tiles. Far away she could spot a small remote. She wondered whom this belonged to. Just then Lathor and Kireb entered the room too. They all stood beside each other and stared at it. Just then they heard the laugh of someone. It was too loud. It was sure that they were in some sort of trouble. The voice was a man's. No one knew what was happening. Everyone had a worried expression.

"What's going on?" Saynna asked.

"I don't know." Kireb replied.

The voice was now getting even louder than before. They thought to turn back and leave the cave but it was too late. The doorway was closed and turned into a wall like the rest. There wasn't even a single mark of the doorway. The tension among them grew and they started to sweat.

"Any alternate?" asked Lathor who kept silent for so long.

"This was a trap. Who would've done this?" questioned Saynna.

"We have all of Lord Rak's men searching for us and I think they have succeeded to do so. I suspect it was a portal. So now no longer are we in White Lake, we are somewhere else. We might be close to Lord Rak's territory too." Nerille replied and then squeezed Saynna's and Lathor's hands tightly.

"That's good news." Saynna said being a bit foolish.

"Saynna we can die. We are in danger." Lathor said.

They were so perplexed. At last an old man showed up near the throne; he emerged out from the ceiling which was weird, but common while struck in a problem like that. He was still laughing aloud. He looked so much like a monster with those wrinkles than a human. He was bald and wore blue robes and blue—gold jewelry. He was perfect for an evil monster god especially with his laugh. It was so cruel. They wondered if anyone would have thought him a as god.

"Who are you?" Saynna asked the old man.

"Me." He answered.

He continued laughing again. Saynna got frustrated by his behavior. He was showing a lot of pride in his words. She felt like attacking him, but resisted her urge as he would be the only one to know where the exit is.

"Who are you?" she asked with a higher pitch this time.

"Me. I wonder why you didn't recognize me. I am indeed the very person your friend thought to meet. I am Dwiedus—the first sea god."

Meeting a god was different. It was their first time too. Saynna never expected a god to look like him. They all paced forward. They were as close as ten yards and could see how big the throne was. Even Dwiedus was the size of his throne. He looked like a giant indeed. Saynna and her mates were just the size of mice in front of him. They felt so puny and helpless too if he would try to attack them.

"Why are you laughing?" Lathor asked who was quite annoyed by it.

"Me? You will know within a while. I see that Manemoore has searching for Hyde. If so, he is with me."

"WHAT?" Saynna and others asked together. They couldn't believe it. "Can we see him?" asked Nerille.

She wanted to see the proof. She didn't know why a god would kidnap a boy who was leading them to save the world though they didn't know how. It was strange. What would a god have to do with him?

"I saw a creature take him. I suppose you are not that creature. You are a god who takes care only of water and not Creatures. It is a part of Haies's duty. I suppose you both are siblings aren't you?" Lathor said without even waiting for the god's response.

"Who said you that Haies is taking care of creatures?" he asked.

It sounded strange to them. Why would a god ask such a question in that situation?

"I am the god of creatures and also the god of water. Lord Rak indeed gave me those powers too." He replied.

"WHAT? How can a sorcerer give powers to a god?" Nerille asked.

"A sorcerer can call a god or goddess for a war. It would be hard to decide who would win then. I was astonished to find out that Lord Rak won. He gave her powers to me and is a prisoner of me."

"Great, but can we see Imas?" she asked for a second time. Previous time there was no response; this time at any cost she did want a response.

"Yes, but you have a lot to do before it."

"Sorry, we didn't get you." Saynna replied.

"It is indeed hard for you but actually at present I am working for Lord Rak as signed in an agreement. He mentioned that if I wanted the powers, I have to capture you and send you to him. That is why I took over Imas."

"What are you talking about? This is too much. Why are most in favor of him? I just wish he dies as soon as possible. I would be rather pleased if I would be the one to kill him." Saynna said.

Dwiedus's smile faded away. His face turned red. They didn't know why he getting red but knew one thing that he got angry. It stated that he was very short tempered.

"Dare you say that!" he warned her.

"Now for the last time can we see Imas?" Nerille shouted.

This time he picked his remote and pressed a blue button on it. Suddenly a cage emerged in the air. It was floating at the far end of the room. They could make out a figure of Imas.

"Imas!" They shouted all together.

Chapter-14

Now that they found him, they had to think of an escape plane because they knew he was a threat as he turned out to be a minion of Lord Rak. Their first priority would be to release Imas from his cage and then try to open a portal or convince him to leave them which of course would not be done by him.

Kireb tried to run towards Imas but was stopped by Dwiedus. He threw his staff at him and he fell backwards. His staff was simple in blue but was powerful. After hitting Kireb, the staff returned to him. Nerille along with Lathor and Saynna ran to him. He was hurt and was also bleeding a bit. Nerille took a small potion which she brought with her and then gave to Kireb.

"Drink this." She said and handed him the colorless potion.

He took it as told and then drank a sip of it. It was so bitter that he spat out a bit of it. The again he tried and this time he was successful. He wiped his mouth and also the blood and then thanked Nerille.

"What did you think you were doing? Can we go out from here along with our friend Imas?" Saynna asked.

"No!" He replied and then continued, "You can leave this place if you want to but I will not send Imas with you. If you want him, you have to cross some impossible things."

"What are those things?" Lathor asked.

"First do you accept you wouldn't want to go without Imas?" Dwiedus queried and put up a smile which meant that he was pleased to have his work done.

"Yes." Nerille replied.

He laughed and then pressed a red button on it. Slowly the tiles beneath them started to rumble.

"An earthquake is it?" Lathor questioned.

"No, it is my Game platform. Step aside contestants. My terror of hell is ready for a game." He said.

"Terror of hell?" Lathor asked with a sickened feeling.

Saynna grabbed Lathor and Nerille along with Kireb and stepped aside as soon as possible. Within a second, they were shocked to see the game platform. It looked so impossible. They doubted if they would cross it and reach Imas.

There were several huge gigantic axes in front of them, swinging to slay off heads. Underneath it was molten magma. There were a few blocks like skipping stones floating from one side to another irregularly along with the axes above them. If they were to go in groups it was impossible. At least one or two would die. So they had to think of freeing Imas by any other means.

"You want us to go in there?" Saynna asked.

"Yes."

"How can we? We will get killed." Kireb replied.

He thought for a while and then and answered, "You don't know the rules, do you?"

"What rules?" Nerille inquired.

"This is just the first round. Second round will be even more dangerous and so will be third one. You have to get ready for worst things." He said.

"Dwiedus don't you have any mercy towards us? You are a bets god. You are the eldest Sea god. Mercy us lord. Please." Lathor requested.

"Mercy?" Saynna asked and continued, "Why should we beg him?"

"Saynna shut up for a while. Please. Lord care not about her. Please . . ."

Lathor got interrupted by Dwiedus. It was suspicious to Dwiedus as all of a sudden Lathor called him 'Lord'. Yet he said, "Fine, I shall give you an offer. You don't have to go in there together. Each one can attempt a round. You decide who shall attempt which round. As you are a group of four, the fourth one will have to face a quiz. Now decide yourselves. If you wish the quiz can be taken off. Now make your decisions. You have one minute to discuss."

"Thank you." Kireb replied.

Kireb was still not very good enough to do anything. They all gathered and started discussing.

"One of us is safe, so who will that be? Lathor asked.

"According to me, I think Kireb has to stay back. He doesn't look fit for these dangerous things." Lathor said.

"Yes. You are right Lathor." Nerille replied.

"No, it's all right. I will take part." Kireb said.

"No. Please we don't have much time. Let us think who would go for the first round."

They thought for a while. It looked so impossible that any person would die with their first step on it. But as the sea god mentioned, the first round is the easiest one, Saynna thought to go for it.

"I'll go for first round as Dwiedus mentioned that it is the easiest one. I suppose I can do it as it might match with my ability." Saynna said.

"Then Lathor shall go for the second round and I will go for the third round. Kireb will warn us at times when we are in danger. Now we will have to be as careful as possible. And . . ."

"Time up!" Dwiedus said.

"Saynna is going for the first round and Lathor for the second round. I am going for the third one."

"Good choice." The sea god said.

"Get ready. Manemoore step up on the dais near the start." He warned.

Saynna started to shiver. In front of her were axes swinging. The next platform was floating a bit far from her.

"Start now!"

Saynna looked for the platform which was coming close to her. She thought to jump but had to look out for the axes. She observed the platforms and axes above it. She found out one thing that the axes were swinging a feet above the platforms. Now that she found an answer to that game she felt it easy. All she had to do was to bend as soon as she jumps from one platform to another. She counted all the platforms and estimated it to be around nine. She closed her eyes and thought about her father for a while and then looked for her friends. They were sweating due to tension. She managed a smile and then turned her attention towards the game. She took a deep breath and as soon as a platform came so close to her, she bent down and rolled on to the other one. Nerille, Lathor and Kireb were all shocked to see her intelligence.

"Good work Saynna!" they shouted.

Dwiedus was also amazed by her intelligence. He didn't know if she would cross at least one platform. He wanted to increase the level of the platforms; hence he pressed another button on his remote.

"Good, keep it up Manemoore." He commented.

Saynna didn't know why he was being so considerate. She tried to move to the next platform which was near her.

"Saynna go for the next one." Kireb advised.

"Yes, do what your friends have told." Dwiedus said.

"What?" Saynna asked in between of her game forgetting about the next Platform. It came so close and so did the axe.

"What is happening lord?" Lathor asked finding a change in the height of the platform and the axe. The space was decreasing.

"Nice game. This will add up tension to you. As she unlocked the game's secret why should I be merciful? I am decreasing the space level in them. I suppose Saynna has to make a choice of dying in molten magma or getting slayed off by axes." Dwiedus answered.

"This is injustice!" Nerille shouted.

"What is?"

"Please lord . . ." Kireb requested.

"Everything is fair in war and war." Dwiedus said.

Meanwhile the time was closing for Saynna slowly the space was reducing and unluckily she missed her next platform she had to wait a while for it to return but until then she had no hope if she would make it.

"Farewell Manemoore." Dwiedus said and waved his hand.

"Saynna beware!" warned Imas from the far corner within his cage. She had to do it for his sake at the least. She thought and thought and last she got an idea. She looked at the axe which was about to slay her and then she jumped off the platform.

"Saynna!" They shouted together.

"Now that is what I was talking about."

"You cheater, you shall pay for this." Nerille cursed.

Dwiedus laughed and then took his remote and pressed a green button on it. After a while, a screen appeared.

"Now let us take a look at your friend's death in a bigger screen." He said and then turned on the screen.

He unlocked the first view. With the first view they could see nothing but the lava boiling.

"Looks like it is too late to see her burn to death. Don't worry, let us rewind." He said.

He pressed the rewind button on it. Before a minute, there was no sign of Saynna. Before one and a half minute too there was no sign of her. Two minutes before too it was the same. Dwiedus got too perplexed.

"Where is she?" he asked to himself.

He then locked the first view. He unlocked the second view. The second too showed the same view. He wondered where she disappeared all of a sudden without even falling into the lava or getting slayed by the axe.

"Where did she disappear?" Kireb asked.

It was desperate for all of them to find her missing. He unlocked the third and the fourth view together. This time they did see Saynna. She was hanging to the platform.

"Oh Saynna you are so clever. Keep up. I am pleased to find someone like you." Nerille said.

"Awesome." Lathor cheered her up.

Dwiedus got frustrated by her intelligence. He had to admit that she was clever and that they were going to take Imas too along with them.

"Saynna be careful. Try not to slip." Lathor warned.

'Try not to slip.' It was stopping her idealistic flow. What if she tripped off or what if she might not reach the next platform.

"Why did you have to remind me that I can slip or trip? You are increasing my worries." Saynna replied.

She was almost half her way. All she had to do was to maintain the balance. If she would succeed in that, she would reach Imas within no time. She was on the fifth platform. The sixth platform was situated a bit far. She had to try her best to make it till there. She took a deep breath and then made a long jump. It was curios for all to watch. Their hearts were beating faster than ever including Dwiedus himself.

Luckily she made it. Within a second, she was slipping. Her friend's worst thoughts were about to come true. Just then an axe got hooked with her dress. She too started to swing along with it. She had no idea when she would fall into the boiling lava. She didn't have any support except for her dress hooked to the axe.

"Aaaaaaaaaaaah!" she screamed.

"Saynna try to jump on the platform or try to reach for another axe." Lathor suggested.

She tried to jump on a platform but she wouldn't succeed especially with another axe swinging near it. She thought for another clever idea as she used to do. Her brain lit up. She knew that she can hang like before. All she had to do was to cut her dress part stuck to the hook at the correct time and position.

"Saynna don't take any wrong decision." Kireb warned.

She saw for the platform. According to her calculations, she had to jump exactly a second before the axe levels with the platform. She took a knife inserted in her pocket.

"It's not fair to have weapons in a game." Dwiedus said.

The rest turned towards him and said, "Everything if fair in love and war or war and war as told."

Saynna cut off the part of her dress hooked at the perfect time and position. She wished herself the best and then within a while she was in the air. She was actually exactly above the platform.

"All the best!" Nerille wished her at the last moment.

She caught hold of the platform with her hand and hanged for it. It was mind blowing for the rest. She then advanced to the next platform and then to the next and at last she hanged to the last platform. One more jump and the she would win and also reach Imas. She made her last jump to the other side dais and she won.

"You win. But don't get too excited, the second and third rounds are waiting for you. As told they are even more dangerous. Now let's begin the second round!" He said.

Chapter-15

It was unbelievable they themselves. For a moment they thought that she might lose. Once they knew that she was safe, they were glad. They were happy that at least one of them is safe and sound. They didn't know what awaited them in the third round. They were confused with their own feelings as on one hand one of them was safe and on the other and as Dwiedus mentioned, the next was to be even more difficult than the previous one. Lathor had not much hope within him. He couldn't imagine anything at that moment. It was he who was going to the next round.

Meanwhile Dwiedus packed up his game platform via his remote and then pressed another red button.

"This round is all about intelligence." Dwiedus said.

'*Oh no!*' Lathor thought.

The only thing that Lathor was afraid of was coming true. He couldn't manipulate faster regarding intelligence. He just wished for that it would be somewhat around his ability.

Dwiedus opened up a whole new platform. This time he opened a pool or some kind of doorway to an ocean.

"What is this?" Nerille asked.

"Good question. It is the second round." He answered.

"We do know it. I am asking you about the second round set up." Nerille said.

"Oh, I was coming to that point. Don't rush me."

The game platform this time was different. It didn't show any kind of threat. The water too was calm without any current influencing its flow. There were no fishes too. It looked odd but the water didn't belong to any ocean nor river or sea but was vast enough for all kinds of fishes. Lathor felt it a bit odd but left to think about it. He wasn't sure if it was some kind of code to unlock his difficulty. He was thinking about it until he was interrupted by Dwiedus.

"Your objective in this round is to find something for me within these depths. This time you have timer too. You have five minutes to complete this task." He warned and then gestured Lathor to stand near the entrance to the water.

Lathor did so as told. He didn't know why but he was shivering badly. He thought it might have been because of cold but it was his fear against winning. Now the only thing he wanted to do was to go home. He didn't any of this going around him. But he very well knew that it was he who accepted to go along with them. He knew how rough their journey would be and yet he got courage. He was brave then, but now he was afraid. Though there was no sign of threat, he felt that something was waiting for him within the waters. He knew that he wasn't quite intelligent and when it came to the fact that this was an intelligent game, he had no hope. A game of intelligence for sure meant that there is something invisible, waiting to be turned visible by the player. He had to crack the code long before searching for what he had to get. There was nothing in there to count on. The water too showed no sign of anything for Dwiedus.

"Wait. Can I take any advice from Haies?" Lathor asked.

"Well, no." he replied.

Lather caught a quick glimpse of Saynna. She was holding Imas's hand and was trying to give him some warmth. He was in water for so long and was also brought here by a creature within the water. So it meant that he came from the water that was below him. The water he was about to pop into. If the creature brought him here, then it must have been in there. It was indeed all that was going on in Imas's head. He was trying his best to crack something and well he was almost up to it. He was sure that there was something inside but didn't it. He thought that for a while until Dwiedus started the count down for him. This Lathor wanted to go in along with his shirt because he was shivering. He turned to Nerille and signaled her to warn him if there was anything that he had to know. Nerille nodded.

"Three . . . two . . . one." He announced.

As soon as he was done with his countdown, Lathor thought to jump in but was afraid that if the water was cold, he would freeze to death. it was really silly for him to think like that but at that time any kind of threats would do. He also expected the water to be too hot or what if the water was electrified?

"Go on!" Kireb shouted.

Lathor knew that his time was getting up. He had to rush. Just to ensure that the water was normal he slid his finger into the water and whirled it. There was no effect and he was glad. He then got up and was about to judge when Nerille called over to him.

"Wait; there is something in the water. Do that again and with more force and check if there are some invisible things."

He bent down and did that again and with a larger force as Nerille told him to do. This time he saw some red rays passing irregularly. Those rays were all over.

"See, that was what I was talking about." Nerille told.

When the water came back to its position, that is staying still, the rays became invisible.

"Do you know what it is?" Lathor asked.

"No." she replied.

He looked around for any object that he could use. He saw a stone nearby. He picked it and threw it in the water. Just when the rays touched it, the stone started to burn. At that instance he knew one thing that if he would have jumped in, he would no longer be present there. He thought of thanking Nerille later and that is when he would do it, which he was doubtful about. He takes a clear view of the water bed and sees a few rocks. One of them looked a bit weird. He was thinking about it when Dwiedus said, "Three more minutes. You better rush."

As soon as Imas heard that, he picked up a stick nearby and then waved the water with his hand and then he slowly slid the stick into areas where there were no red evil rays passing on. When the water was becoming still, he waved it again and then pushed it deeper and deeper till he reached the rock which he felt was mysterious. He poked it twice and to his wonder, the rock was not hard. It was soft and got impaled by his stick. He went on pushing his stick till he felt that it pushed something. Indeed the stick was so long. When he first saw it, it was of medium size. Then when he started to push it deeper it started to extend. He didn't know how it happened but it was amazing.

He pushed something inside the soft rock that he couldn't see it. After a second or so the rays became visible to naked eye without having to wave the water. He felt happy for it. He then threw the stick and slowly started to get into the water and swam without getting caught by the rays. Now that the fact that he got to know how to get inside, the next thing he had to do was to search for a thing for Dwiedus.

"Two more minutes. Time is getting up. Don't think that now you can easily accomplish your task." Dwiedus said.

He better rush. He thought about an object that is fancied by a sea god. He thought and thought as he made his way through the red rays. Pearls! That's it. It was royal symbol for sea gods or goddess's. He heard this several times from Nerille when she was trying to teach him about the history of Icewilde. Then he thought how boring it was. But now he felt like thanking her as soon as he goes out. Only if he made it within time, then would he stand a chance to thank her twice. Once for warning him not to jump into the water. Second time she saved him by teaching him about the likes and dislikes of gods, especially sea gods and goddess. It was an indirect help though.

He looked around and spotted a spotless white shining rock. It was not well cut, but looked really good and was an exact replica of a pearl. He picked it up and slowly turned back. He started to leave for the entrance.

"One minute to end the round."

He got nervous. He didn't know if he would make it or not but promised himself not to rush as he would be burnt to death. He felt something behind him. It was some kind of sound that was made by monsters. *Monsters!*

He didn't know why a monster showed up after so long, when he was almost done with his task. He cursed the monster. The monster too was invisible. It was hard for him to make out the monster. Without even turning back, he made his way to the entrance.

"What are you doing?"

He heard Nerille's voice. He felt as though she was debating with someone. Of course it had to be Dwiedus. He was the only one who was their opponent. Opponent in the case the one who was making them fall into troubles. Lathor swore that once he is done with this, he would kill the god. He knew that it was impossible to kill a god. If any person of Icewilde kills a god, it was to be termed that he would start the dark days. He didn't know how or why someone would want to start the dark days even by knowing its result.

Dark days were considered as a threat to everyone. It was very much related to Lord Rak. The dark days can only be started by a person who has killed a god or goddess. It would release the powers of Lord Rak. And by the powers, it meant Lord Rak's original powers.

Meanwhile Lathor was struggling to get out of the water before the monster catches him and also before the time is out.

"Thirty seconds . . ."

He hears from Dwiedus. Tension was growing. He tried to act normal as if he didn't see any signs of the monster.

"Stop it!" Nerille said.

"What can I do?" Dwiedus replied.

"You are ridiculous!" Nerille shouted.

Hearing that, one thing was clear to Lathor that Dwiedus was cheating again. *'Why can't the gods stay without cheating small innocent kids?'* He thought. He was feeling totally helpless then.

When he was about to reach the surface, the monster caught him from back. It tried to pull him. If he would try to escape, he would burn to death as there were rays all over. He slowly thought of Haies. She was indeed the only other goddess who was in favor with them. He didn't know if she would have supported them if she wasn't in prison. He thought about her and her duty. He thought about the injustice done to her.

Suddenly the cage of Haies along with Haies within it appeared in front of him. He was shocked.

"So you are Haies?" he asked.

"It is no time for introductions. While leaving this fort, promise me that you will also release me. If you do that, I shall use all my power on it to stop it. Now, do you agree?" she questioned.

"Deal." I replied.

Haies looked charming apart from being a monster goddess. She had lovely eyes and beautiful long hair which was black. She was wearing a gray gown not too fancy.

"Thanks." He said.

He wanted her at least to feel that he was grateful. Haies chanted something. He wasn't able to hear it. After five seconds or so after chanting, the monsters grip started to loosen. As soon as he felt that, he started to swim quickly, keeping in mind about the rays.

"Three . . . two."

He came out of the water along with the stone just when Dwiedus said, "One and time up."

Nerille felt a relief with her only to find out that next was her chance. Lathor himself wasn't able to believe that he had made it within time.

"You were late." Dwiedus said.

"WHAT?" they asked together.

It was clear that he was out by the time Dwiedus said '*Time up!*'

"You can see it by yourselves."

He then pressed a button on the remote and the screen came into view. He unlocked the first view and played the part when Lathor was getting out. He slowed the motion to catch a clear view. '*Two . . . One . . .*"

He was out when Dwiedus said, '*One and time up!*"

Now it was clear to everyone that Lathor had done his round perfectly. But there was something else to prove him if he has made it or not.

"Show me what you have brought." Dwiedus asked.

Lathor began to shiver. It was due to both the reasons—cold, tension. He looked at the rock and turned it in his hands.

"Quick, give it to me now." He ordered.

"Well, will you promise me something?"

"What?" Dwiedus queried.

Lathor thought not to ask about it then.

"Nothing." He ended up.

"Tell me what it is at the instant." He said.

"I said nothing!" he shouted.

He didn't want to shout but ended up shouting. Dwiedus's face got red. He was boiling with anger.

"I'm sorry. It is nothing." He replied.

He then handed the stone to Dwiedus. Dwiedus too turned the stone in his hands forgetting about Lathor's misbehavior. He examined it for a minute and then said, "Pearl."

Lathor was pleased that it was a pearl, a secret favor of Dwiedus. He felt glad but the decision that would be made by Dwiedus after a while was giving him Goosebumps.

"You did it." He announced.

He felt really happy for it. From far away Saynna too looked happy. Their team was doing well. But he hadn't yet forgotten the reason how he had won. It was all because of Haies. He yet didn't know how he was going to release her. Beside him, Nerille had a worried expression stating that it was her chance next.

"Now, let the third round begin." He said with a cruel smile on his face.

Chapter~16

Now it was Nerille's turn to prove her. After Saynna and Lathor being outstanding at their wits, Nerille also thought that she might do it. She indeed found confidence as well as over confidence that she might do it. There was no tension or force acting upon her to get tensed and act quickly.

"Now, my turn." She says to herself.

She expected the maze to be dependent on something possible by her. She looks at Dwiedus and asks him to bring up her round. She was sure that it had nothing to do with intelligence as one round was already based upon it. Dwiedus looks at her confirmation and Nerille nods.

"This round is based on everything." Dwiedus said.

'*Great!*' Nerille thought.

It was a perfect idea to mess with her. She focused on his expressions but he was expressionless except for his cruel smile which was always present. She wanted to find an answer hidden in his face, but no use. Lathor looked quite overjoyed. He had no more worries. She turned to Kireb who was getting better. Nerille cursed Dwiedus for harming him.

"Do you have any rules or guidance for my game?" Nerille asked.

Dwiedus looked around and then turned to her and answered, "Your game? This is my game. And coming to the game, you will have no timer or any threats."

Nerille felt a relief within her. Now that there were no threats for her, it was going to be easy for her. There was no timer too which meant that she could take a lot of time and not rush. There were many probabilities of her winning. But there was one fear within her. Dwiedus said that the third round would be even more difficult than the first two rounds. She wondered in what way her round was going to be that difficult.

"So what is the round all about?" Nerille queried.

"I already told you." Dwiedus replied.

"What? That was not exactly an explanation for the round. You gave more details for the other rounds." She reasoned.

Dwiedus told nothing but went on pressing some weird buttons on his remote. Nerille wondered how a remote could handle so many things as it was her first time to watch someone do that especially a god. It was weird for her. After a second a table emerged from the floor with many vials. There were some weird liquids within it. Potions! That was a perfect test for her. She was an expert in potions no matter whatever kind it was of.

'*That's easy!*" Nerille thought.

"Don't you think that!" Dwiedus warned.

"What? You read my thoughts. Could you do that?" Nerille asked.

It was strange. She never thought that god could read someone's mind. She thought not to think any solution especially in front of him as he cheated a lot. She hated him a lot.

"I already did that." Dwiedus answered.

"It is not fair. Don't you think that you should ask permission? God's too must need to learn manners."

Dwiedus just ignored her.

"Your round begins now."

"Wait, you haven't yet told me what I have to do." Nerille said.

Dwiedus doesn't pay her attention and Nerille gets confused on what she had to do.

"Look, this completely not fair. You tell me at least one thing on what I have to do."

"Now start your round!"

THE LOCKET OF MOONSTONE

Nerille didn't know anything. She just went up to the vials. There were about nine vials or so. Each one had a different colored potion within it. She had to make a different plan all of a sudden as she didn't know what she had to do. She felt despicable. She went up to the first vial. She picked it up and examined the color, which was in blue. She smelled the vial as she removed the cork and when she was done she put it back. It smelled of nothing. That potion was completely a stranger potion for her. She never learned or knew about any potion with a royal blue color that was odorless.

"Where did you get these potions? They are so weird."

"You need not care about it." Dwiedus replied.

"One more thing, what are these potions for?" Nerille asked though she knew that he won't answer.

"You must know that these are potions. You also know pretty much about potions. So I need not tell you anything. You just do what you are feeling to do. Remember that if you fail, you shall stay back."

'Stay back?' Nerille thought.

She never failed in anything especially in a potion test. If anyone gets to know about this, she felt that her career would be in vain. Thought there was no connection between her and her village, she yet supported them. She felt that just because they ignored her, didn't mean that they didn't want her. She would always be there for her foes. From her childhood, she remembered her mother telling her that,

"United we stand,
Divided we fall."

Remembering that, she felt some kinds of hint stroke her. She thought of processing her thoughts for the answer but she forgot. She then left that thought, and went up to the second vial. It was of turquoise color. It too smelled of nothing.

"Why do the potions smell of nothing?"

Dwiedus banged his head to his staff.

"You are indeed impossible. Can you please keep one thing in your mind that you are playing a game. Did I not mention you that you must drink a potion?" Dwiedus blurted out unknowingly.

That gave a complete push up for her.

"Thank you." Nerille replied.

'Oh no!' Dwiedus thought.

It was indeed clever of Nerille to confuse and irritate him to give her a hint. She tried to do it from the first without keeping this in her thoughts as Dwiedus knew how to read other's minds.

Nerille goes to the third one. It was green in shade. The next one was yellow. The fifth one was of orange shade. The next one was of red shade. The seventh one was black in shade. The next was pale white. The last one was colorless.

After observing all those shades of potions, Nerille had to decide upon one vial. The first was blue a shade of the sea and so was the second one. Sometimes it could also be colorless. So she was left with three choices. Which one should she drink? First one or second one, or the third one?

In spite of tricking him for once, she thought of doing it for another time.

"Dwiedus, why are there so many vials. Can the unwanted ones be eliminated? If so please do it."

"Look, if I was fooled for once doesn't mean that the trick would work for another time. Try something else, traitor."

Nerille felt angry. She was so helpless. She encouraged everyone, but coming to her round, there was no one giving her any suggestions.

Now that she was on her own, she decided to go through her thoughts for some help.

'United we stand,
Divided we fall.'

That was it! She figured it out that instead of drinking one she can drink all. Maybe they were all divided. They were supposed to be a single potion but were separated by some magical process that she didn't know. She wanted an extra vial for mixing all of them and then drinking it. She was so glad and happy that her round would be over in less than a while as soon as she gets a vial.

"Dwiedus, can I get an extra empty vial?"

"No. I am afraid you would have to use only the ones given to you. Now, please try not to ask me anymore questions. I must admit that you are indeed the most talkative girl I have ever seen." He replied.

Nerille now had to figure out a way by which she can drink all together. She felt that this god was useless. She thought for a while and at last she got an idea. She thought that she would drink potions one after another. She felt that it would be the same.

She went back to the first vial and drank it. As soon as it was swallowed she went to the second one and drank it. She followed this method until all the vials were empty.

"Dwiedus, have I passed the test?" Nerille asked.

Dwiedus laughed.

"Does that mean that we can all go to Blackdell?"

He gave no reaction except for his laugh.

"Dwiedus answer me."

He didn't pay her any attention by which she got angry.

"You will know that within a while." He said plainly.

Nerille didn't get his point. She turned to Kireb and Lathor. They too had no reaction or any expression. Far away she could see Saynna and Imas. They were looking forth for her victory which would be announced any moment. They were sure that she had done the right thing.

Just then she felt some kind of force acting upon her to sleep. Her vision was getting dizzy. She tried to overcome that feeling but couldn't help it. Her eyelids were getting heavy and then she slowly started to lose her balance.

"Nerille are you all right?" Kireb asked.

Nerille turned to Kireb. She observed that he was completely fit then. She wanted to tell him that she wanted some sleep.

"Dwiedus what is wrong with Nerille?" questioned Lathor.

"You wait and see."

Her body was no longer following her commands.

"Dwie . . . dus . . ." She managed but failed to complete her sentence.

She was about to fall when Kireb and Lathor ran to her. They caught her just in time. She fainted indeed.

"Dwiedus, what happened to her?" Lathor asked.

He was delighted to see her fail the round. He was glad.

"She failed the round and I won." He said.

'*Failed the round?*' Lathor thought.

"Is she safe?" Kireb asked.

"You can find out." He replied.

Lathor and Kireb checked her heartbeat and found out that she was breathing. It meant that she was alive. They were at least happy that she was alive but were also unhappy that she failed the round. Now their fates were dependent on Dwiedus, an evil sea god.

"What now? Can we please go along with Nerille?" Lathor queried.

"No! You will have to leave her here. She failed the round and has fallen asleep. She will be asleep forever. Now you are leaving this place without her or stay here with me. The choice is yours.

"We leave this place." Kireb answered without even considering anything about Nerille.

"What? We cannot leave Nerille here." Lathor said.

"What about your quest? If you want to accomplish the quest for Imas and Saynna, we have to leave now. We shall come here again to release her. I promise you that Nerille will be safe here. He has no work with her. Now let's go. It is getting late for us."

"Well then you are leaving now."

As soon as Dwiedus said that, Nerille's body started to rise. Then after a while a glass covered her and then she disappeared.

'*Farewell Nerille.*' Lathor thought.

"Good bye kids. Get ready to go to the doors of the death." Dwiedus said and then he tapped his finger and then after a while the whole scene disappeared.

They were no longer in the province of the sea god. They were on an island. It was none other than the Whitelake.

Chapter-17

Sun was stretched upon the valley. They could hear birds chirping. The bird's voices were so refreshing, especially after having a bad time playing a game. They heard the sound of the water crashing stones. It was an admirable scene for a holiday visit, but it was their bad luck that they had to rush.

"Nice place." Saynna complimented.

They sat on the grass for a while. Saynna was happy that Imas was back, but at the same time she felt sorry for Nerille. It was strange for a potion expert to fail in a potion test. But as Nerille stated that those potions were quite new to her, there were probabilities of her to lose and she did. Saynna badly wanted Nerille to win. But it was done. Now no matter what she thought, there would be no more changes made.

"Feeling bad for her?" Imas asked.

He looked healthy. He was not weak any more. It looked like a miracle to Saynna. She doubted how it happened. She had one guess, which she thought was lame. She thought that Dwiedus put him under a spell which got broken after he left Dwiedus's premises.

"Yes. What about you? How were you so long? What exactly happened?" She questioned him.

"Well, I bet you know until the part I was kidnapped by the monster. Then, I fainted. When I woke up, I was in a cage. And then I was so tired or maybe he put me under a spell, I don't know which exactly. After a few minutes a person shows up, and then did I know that it was Dwiedus—the sea god. He told me all about himself, and then he goes away. Later, my cage and I appear in the game room or punishment chamber of his. I was pleased to find you all over there, and later you do know what happened. When you were playing, I was so tensed. I didn't know why but my heart stopped when you jumped off from the platform at once. Anyway it is all over now, but I do feel bad for her."

"Glad you are back." She said.

"Yeah, even me." he replied.

Lathor and Kireb were near a stream. They were trying to catch a fish with a stick. Looking at that scene, Imas and Saynna started to feel hungry. They too forgot that almost a day has passed and that they ate nothing so long. They stared at Lathor and Kireb for any food. They did show some signs of luck. Lathor was holding a fish and Kireb caught two fishes.

"What do you think?" Imas asked.

"Let's go!" she replied.

They got up and went to Lathor and Kireb.

"Shall we cook them?" Saynna asked.

Saynna cooked the fishes with the help of fire lighted by Imas. The twigs were good enough to light a fire as they lasted for so long. Once the cooking was done, Saynna shared with them. They were pleased to eat it. Within a few minutes their meal was done.

"Nice one. Thanks for cooking them Saynna!" Kireb complimented.

"You're welcome."

"So, what is the backup plan?" Lathor asked.

Imas didn't want to answer but he couldn't resist them.

"We reach Blackdell by tomorrow and then we release my mother and Saynna's father. Then they will help us to find the heir of Ragnarok, which would give us an answer to the problem."

"But Imas I think you told me that your mother was killed by Lord Rak?" Saynna said.

"Yes, but recently I got to know that she is alive and that she is in Blackdell with your father."

"But how do you know? There weren't any messages recently."

"I got to know this through a dream of mine." He replied.

He wanted to keep this as a secret but as the plan had to be discussed he had to disclose.

"That sounds insane. How can you tell which one of your dreams is true?" Lathor questioned.

"I had a feeling that tells that she is still alive."

Kireb put a confused expression. He felt that their plan was stupid. He only knew that he had to drop them at Blackdell. Hence he left to think about their plan. He went on listening to them.

"Anyway when do we start?" asked Lathor.

"Now." Imas replied.

"Don't you think we should rest for a while?" Saynna asked.

"According to me your father and my mother are going to die by tomorrow night. Hence our deadline is closing and we have to leave this place at once."

After he said that he got up and started to leave for the boat. Saynna and Lathor too followed him. Kireb thought for a while and then he too followed them. He had no idea in which direction they came.

They reached the shore within a while of walking. It was pleasant. This place looked beautiful, but wasn't exactly. It was a killer land. They were pleased that at last they were leaving this dangerous island.

"Where do you think is the ship?" Lathor asked.

"I don't know." Saynna replied.

They turned their attention to Kireb. Looking at their stares at him, he was sure that they relied upon him.

"According to me, it must be there . . ." he said pointing front.

"Are you sure?" They asked together.

"Do you have any other alternate?" Kireb replied.

They looked away in another direction. Kireb started going and the rest did follow him.

"Look, there it is!" Saynna shouted.

She was right. They could spot a figure far away from them that resembled a ship. They started to rush. After a few minutes they reached the ship. They were so happy.

"Hello!" Kireb said to the ship.

He then started to board the ship. He slowly climbed the ladder as if he was checking its ability. When he was on-board, he called the others to come up. They too started climbing the ladder one after another. First it was Saynna, then Imas and at last Lathor.

"Good to be back." Imas said.

Saynna headed to her cabin and then collapsed on the bed. Imas and Lathor too did the same. Kireb went straight to do his duty.

"Wait, are you going without releasing me?" said a voice out of nowhere.

Lathor froze at once. The voice was a woman's and sounded familiar to him. He turned to Imas. He showed no reaction. Lathor expected it to be his mind playing tricks because even Imas behaved as though he didn't hear anything.

"You are not doing this to me. If you do so, the reactions later would be violent. Tell me Lathor what do you think you are doing, forgetting about me?" She asked him again.

Lathor didn't know what this woman was speaking about or why she was talking only to him.

"Imas, do you hear that?" He asked to confirm.

"Hear what?"

By this it was clear to him that he was the only one listening to her. He really had no idea about what was going on.

"Don't you recognize me?" the woman asked.

"Who are you? You sound familiar." He said at last as a response to her.

"What are you talking about Lathor?" Imas asked.

"Wait for a while . . ." he said and continued, "I am not talking to you."

Imas kept quite as told.

"Answer me lady." He said.

Imas felt that something was happening without him knowing. He was sure that someone was talking to Lathor secretly through the mind.

"What happened to you? Are you still there?" Lathor questioned.

"Yes. You do know me very well. I helped you but what did I get in return? I didn't get anything. By this I am sure that you would know who I am." She said.

"Can you please be straight forward?" He requested.

"I am your savior. There is no one who doesn't know me. Try to remember what happened a while ago and you will know. I am ashamed to help you."

Lathor thought for a while.

"You . . . you are . . ." He stammered.

"I give it to you. I am Haies—the god of monsters. You promised me that you would release me but what did you do? You didn't even try to release me."

"Haies, I am sorry. I thought that I would ask him after the game was over but I was distracted by Nerille. I promise you that I would come and release you as soon as this is over. Please believe me." Lathor said.

"I would but remember this is your last chance. If you wouldn't release me, I will kill Nerille as she is with me. All the best." She said for one last time.

"No don't do that." He replied.

Their conversation ended as she was no longer speaking. He turned to Imas who very well understood that he was speaking to Haies as he mentioned her name once.

"It was just the thing that I . . ."

Lathor got interrupted by Imas.

"I know. Let's go and check with Kireb."

They left the cabin and went to Kireb.

"How's everything going?" Imas asked.

"I have good news for you. Previously we were not in White lake. We were in some place that is close to Blackdell. Dwiedus transported us to our destination. Why do you think he has done this?" Kireb asked.

"That is indeed good news. I suspect he wants us to land in Lord Rak's territory as fast as possible. Anyway he kind of helped us." Imas said.

"Yes, he did by prompting us to more dangers." Lathor said.

"Anyway, we will be landing within a few hours that are one or two hours. Tell this to Nerille and Saynna too."

"Nerille is no more here Kireb." Lathor reminded.

"Fine, tell it to Saynna." he said and then continued his duty.

"All right then, we shall leave now." Imas said.

They went to Saynna. The door was open so they went in.

"Saynna . . ." Imas called out.

She was sitting staring at the water. Hearing them she got up and paid attention to them.

"We have good news for you." Imas and Lathor said together.

Chapter-18

Saynna was glad to hear that. She was thankful to Dwiedus only for this reason. Now that their destination was close, she was getting tensed. She had a feeling that she would get caught by Lord Rak. But they had to try their only alternate. There were no more decisions to be made as everything was planned.

"That is good. Well then I will take a good nap till then." She said.

"Nice idea." Lathor complimented.

"Bye then." Imas said.

Saynna waved to them and as soon as they left, she closed the door. She dozed off to sleep. She started dreaming.

She saw a woman in black robes standing with a girl. They were facing their backs towards her so she couldn't guess who they were. The woman was telling the girl about Lord Rak.

"He is indeed a person so stubborn about achieving it. I bet you knew about him better than I do, don't you?" The woman said.

"Yes, as he is the one who destroyed my family." The girl replied.

The girl's voice was familiar to Saynna. Nerille! Exactly, it was her voice for sure. She wondered who she was talking to.

"Austaudia, why don't you support your brother?" Nerille questioned.

Saynna had to listen to them though she didn't know what they were talking about. She was only sure about one thing that the woman whom Nerille was talking to was called Austaudia.

"My brother is so evil. My father was so good, but it was my brother who had a problem with him. My mother supported him. Then a fight began and they killed my father. I was so young then. I would have been ten years or so. I had to accept for whatever my mother and brother would tell. Time passed and after a few years, there was Ragnarok who depicted a war and that started everything. Hearing that rumor, people were scared of my brother and mother and me. They thought that we were indeed going to destroy them. By brother took advantage of this situation and began to dominate people. He and my mother together killed anyone who opposed them. I hated them a lot but I couldn't express my feelings because I had a fear that they would kill me. Then within a few years he got an immortality potion and gave to the three of us. Actually I didn't want to live with them but I am forced to do it." She said.

Her voice was so sweet. Now it was clear to her that Lord Rak had a good sister named Austaudia.

"Now I get it. Anyways, don't you get bored over here? You have all minions but no companions. I know how you feel being all alone." Nerille replied.

"I do get bored. Whenever there are any prisoners, I go and talk to them. That is how I keep myself entertained."

"Austadia, I bet you are not known to many, are you?" Nerille asked.

"Yes. I am indeed happy that I am not popular for being an evil lord's sister. So, how are your friends doing?"

'Friends? Here we are entering the doors of death.' Saynna thought.

"I bet they will achieve their goal, and yes, I am sure that they will come and release me later."

"Saynna!" A voice shouted not too far from her.

She slowly opens her eyes and finds out that it was Imas.

"Imas, I locked the door, but how did you come in?" She questioned.

He smiled and helped her to her feet.

"I have my own tricks. After this ends, I will teach you also. This is an important trick to be learned by you."

Saynna too smiled back.

"So, are we there yet?" she asked.

"Yes. We have arrived Blackdell. Indeed it's been a while since we came here. So you ready to go?"

"To get killed? Yes." She replied.

They giggled and then went on to the deck.

"There is something that I want to tell you." Saynna said.

"And what is it?" Imas asked.

"I had a dream. I felt it like a vision just like you told previously."

"Go on." Imas said.

She told him about her dream. Just when she finished, Lathor and Kireb came with their backpacks.

"Ready?" Lathor and Kireb asked.

They handed Saynna and Imas each a backpack.

"We have a companion in there." Imas said.

"Who is it?" Lathor queried.

"Austadia. We have another companion too. It is Nerille. According to Saynna, she is in the palace. This means that we have three people to save from Lord Rak. Another thing is that Lord Rak might know that we are here. Actually he does know." Imas said.

"That is great then." Lathor said.

"Very well then, we go in. We have no particular plan, but as we need one I am telling you. We first enter the fort and then head to the prisons. We search for the three of them." Saynna told.

"But won't it take a lot of time?" Kireb questioned.

"Then we go individually in search of them. When you are exiting the fort, just give a signal." Saynna advised.

"What kind of signal?" Imas asked.

Saynna whistled. The others followed and they agreed for the signal.

"Kireb, you stay here and guard the ship. The rest of us will go looking for them." Imas advised.

"Then we leave at this instance." Imas ordered.

By that the discussion ended and they left. The trio felt a bit tensed but this was the time they had to show their braveness.

"We can do it." Imas encouraged Lathor and Saynna.

"Just try not to get caught." Lathor suggested.

"I completely forgot about the fact that there would be guards over there. Thanks for reminding." Saynna said.

They got down from the ship. The land was so dry and the sky was red. It was a perfect place for someone like Lord Rak to live. They could spot a fort in front of them. It was the back of the fort so they didn't had to hide from the guards. No ever dared to enter his fort except for the prisoners and guards. The fort was very tall about ten floors or so. It was made of rock. It was carved very well. The designs on it showed everything about mortals being suppressed. Looking at that Saynna wanted to punish him.

"Nice work." Lathor complimented.

"Yes, it indeed is for a devil." Imas added.

They rushed to the fort as fast as possible without getting caught. Though there were no guards over there it wasn't safe for them to roam like that in a territory of their enemy.

"We disperse at this movement." Imas said.

They did as told. There were three gates. One was at the starting; one was at the middle, and one at the end. Imas went to the starting one while Saynna chose the middle one. Lathor had to go to the last one for sure as it was the only left out. He took last and final look at Saynna and Imas and then went to his gate. He opened it.

It was the same with others. They also did the same thing. Saynna got tensed and waited out for a while and then went in. It was dark. So, Saynna took a stick nearby and lighted it with matchsticks within her backpack. The tunnel was hollow and was made of metal. There was no sign of anyone over there. She advanced forward slowly and swiftly. She tried hard not to make any kind of sounds. She even controlled the noise made by her footsteps. The complete silence was unbearable by her. She wanted to make some noise or hum a song but she herself knew that if she did that she would be in trouble. She touched the wall and tapped upon it. By her calculations, it was supposed to be collapsing anytime. That was really alarming her. She figured out that it must be the reason why no guards were there. She started rushing at that instance without even caring about the noise made and she being caught. She ran until she reached a forked path. She was supposed to take one of the paths. She took a look at both of the passages. They were the same. She thought and after taking the decision, she went into the path that was situated to the right of her. She began rushing again.

She could spot light not too far from her. She guessed that she was entering the fort and tip-toed till she reached the exit of the tunnel. She stopped a bit back before the exit just to ensure that there was no one. She took a peek and spotted that both the guards were sleeping. She thought herself to be lucky and tip-toed out of the tunnel. She looked around and there no other guards except for the sleeping ones.

She was able to see the first and second prisons. She moved forward and found that it was not any of the three. She never knew that there was a direct entry to the prisons in Lord Rak's fort. She advanced towards the next one and the next one. She went on exploring them but never found any of them in one of those. She rested near a prison for a while.

She heard a noise from behind her. She quickly hid nearby. She waited for anyone to appear but no one came. She stepped out and at once she was standing in front of Kireb. Seeing him all of a sudden she backed away.

"Oh! It is you. You scared me." Saynna whispered to Kireb.

"Yes, it is me."

"Weren't you supposed to stay on the ship?" Saynna asked.

"Yes, but I thought you might need some help searching for them." He said.

He had a cruel smile on his face.

"Never mind." Saynna replied.

Saynna started to go forward. She looked at the last one and she found someone familiar within it. There was a woman in it. She was wearing black robes. She looked very pretty. Saynna suspected it to be some goddess.

"Who are you lady?" Saynna questioned her with a low voice.

"I am Haies." She replied.

"You are a goddess. I will be pleased to release you." she said.

She went and released her by using magic.

"Thank you." Haies replied.

Haies chanted something and then within a few seconds she vanished.

"You did a very wrong thing releasing my prisoner. I shall not spare you."

"What are you talking about? Your prisoner?" Saynna asked.

"Who do you think I am?" Kireb asked.

"Kireb, why are you behaving so strangely? And please lower your voice. We can get caught."

"I am Lord Rak!" He shouted.

Chapter-19

Saynna was shocked. She didn't know until then that her enemy was with her. She couldn't believe that all this long she was with Lord Rak. She trusted him though they weren't supposed to trust anyone and at last she fell in trouble. How could she not have thought that Kireb was none other than their destroyer? Her anger and rage towards him for betrayal was more than anything she could have dreamt of.

"You . . . you . . . it simply can't be." She said though she believed that he was lord Rak.

"Yes, I am indeed your most wanted person. Didn't you at the least have a hint that I am Lord Rak all this long?"

Saynna stayed calm and silent trying to sink in the truth.

"At first, it was me who stopped the boat telling that there was a problem. Next, I was the one who took you to Dwiedus's chamber. Over there he bet me at first only because I had to escape the games. This was my entire plan. You are indeed playing in my game. How foolish of you to plan of killing me when I was with you? Now you have a chance of killing me. Kill me!" He shouted.

Saynna backed off. She was stunned by the truth that revealed. She wanted to run and she did at once ignoring the fact that she was with Lord Rak who is an evil sorcerer.

She ran back to the entrance but Lord Rak who was in the form of Kireb appeared in front of her all at once.

"Trying to get away?" He asked with a sweet voice which Saynna believed wasn't his true form.

He caught hold of her.

"Let me go!" She demanded.

He wouldn't listen to her and started dragging her to one of the prisons. He shoved her in and locked the gate.

Saynna fell hard on the floor. It was the very prison in which Haies was locked. Saynna thought of how she previously released Haies and began to do the same thing again.

"Don't you think of it. The prisoner within can never attempt to perform any magic. You think you are too clever, huh?"

Saynna quit what she was doing and sat on a bench over there that was made of thick branches. Meanwhile Lord Rak, chanted something that sounded like,

> 'Miewa sican thora shewa
> Thete yere soman mewa'

Purple smoke arose from beneath him. It covered him completely. It stayed for a while and then it began to vanish.

As the smoke was going, Saynna could see something weird. It was Lord Rak's original form. He had dark skin, completely opposite to his sister and he had no hair. He was bald. His eyes could easily trick a person as they were so sharp and hypnotizing. He was wearing a red robe with black decorations. He also had a crown with snakes swirling into each other. His staff was not any less. It too was weird as it looked like a snake that was in motion.

"Come here girl!" he ordered.

Saynna slowly got up and went near as she had no other alternate.

"What is it?" she asked.

He took out a chain that he was wearing. Its pendent had two tiny snakes swirling. Lord Rak took out the pendent and opened it. Within it was a pin like object. The next thing he did was he pricked my hand with it. He collected the blood with the help of the pendent.

"Ouch!" Saynna shouted.

She quickly backed away from him.

"Don't worry this is more than enough for changing my form." He said.

He then drank the blood collected in the pendent. After drinking he chanted the previous charm. This time the smoke was red. After it disappeared, Saynna could see herself standing outside the prison.

"This can't be happening. You are me."

"Yes it is happening. I am Saynna Manemoore." Lord Rak said with Saynna's voice.

She was shocked. Lord Rak looked exactly like her. He was to be termed as her replica indeed.

The duplicate Saynna started moving away from the prisons.

"Wait! You can't do this!" She shouted but the duplicate Saynna was no more there.

She sat there all alone thinking about what the rest might be doing.

Chapter~20

Complete silence was maintained. No other noise could be heard except for the sound made by Imas's footsteps. The tunnel was quite long. It was just like the one Saynna went through. Imas walked as slow as he could. After he covered some distance, he heard a noise. He turned back but could see nothing as he was travelling without any light. The only source of light was from the lanterns that were hanging high. He slowly mad another move. The noise was getting closer. This time he concentrated from where the noise was coming and to his amazement he saw something unusual. The tunnel was collapsing. Imas began to run as fast as he could and made it to the entrance just in time.

He felt safe and secured as he reached the prisons. Only the fact that he didn't know what was awaiting him over there.

He slowly tip-toed and went from one prison to another in search of his mother, Saynna's dad and Nerille. He couldn't find any of them. But he carried on his search. He reached the last prison and found Saynna's dad over there. He was very much pleased but was also sad seeing his condition. King Cephas Manemoore was in no condition to walk. Imas had no idea how he would release him and take him somewhere safe.

"Your majesty, I am here to save you." Imas said.

Cephas looked at Imas. He had an expression of happiness in his face. He got up and walked towards the prison bars. He passed his hand between them and took hold of Imas's hand.

"Imas, you cannot save me." He said softly.

"Sir, there is no backing off from here. We are about to reach our destiny." Imas replied.

"Destiny? This is just the beginning of your journey and you talk about destiny?" King Cephas asked Imas.

"Sir we don't have much time. Please tell me how to release you as I am not too good at this."

"You can't release by whatever methods you try to. You have only one way. I will tell you about the heir of Ragnarok. His heir is a farmer and I guess you do know about it. It will take you more time to find him. I have another alternate. You can use any farmer in his place. Ask the farmer to try his best to concentrate on the locket. It will show him something. Follow whatever is shown by the locket and you will achieve to stop him for a while. It would be a temporary lock for him. Meanwhile you can find the original heir and send him to sleep forever. Now, go from here and don't trust anyone. Not even my daughter. Go!" King Cephas ordered.

"But there is no exit except for the tunnel and it's no longer present." Imas said.

"There is one secret passage. Go straight from here and take a left when you reach the dead end. It will lead you to the next tunnel." He said.

As soon as he ended, Imas ran without even wasting any time. He reached the dead end and took a left and reached the next tunnel as told by the King. He stopped when he spotted Lathor over there.

"Lathor!" he whispered.

Lathor too spotted him and then ran to him.

"What is it Imas?" he asked.

"Are you a farmer?" he asked.

"Imas, I have told you that several times. Now what difference does that make?"

Imas's face lit up. He pulled out the locket that was with him and gave it to Lathor. Lathor didn't know what Imas was up to.

"Lathor, I just met Cephas and he said that we can temporarily send Lord Rak to sleep only if you could see what is in there."

Lathor did as told. He concentrated on it for several minutes.

"I don't see anything but for a mirror." Lathor said at last.

"Mirror? Do you have one?" Imas asked.

"Well, no, but the locket has a mirror behind it." He said observing the locket.

"That is it then. We will try to show Lord Rak this mirror and something might happen."

Lathor did not reply. Imas started rushing. Lathor too followed him. They went deeper into the tunnel in which they were standing. They suddenly stopped when they spotted Saynna.

"Saynna! Come along quickly." Lathor shouted.

Saynna ran to them. There was something odd. She was running differently. Her style wasn't the same. But Imas ignored the difference.

"Look at what we have figured out." Lathor said.

Imas showed the mirror to Saynna. The light that fell on her was reflected back. Smoke started rising from Saynna's body.

"What did you do?" Saynna shouted.

Lathor and Imas were also perplexed. They too had no idea about what was going on. Within minutes Saynna's body was vaporized. Then did they understand that Saynna was none other than Lord Rak disguised. It was shocking for them. They thanked their luck. They themselves didn't know how simple it was and they were pleased to have their duty done at least on a temporary basis. But one question arose in their minds, *'Where is Saynna?'* In addition, another question raised, *'What next?'*

The End

Daddala Vineesha Chowdary is a teenage author. She started writing this book when she was 12 years old. She discovered her ability when she first wrote a poem. From then on, she started emphasizing on that skill. One of the reasons about why she wrote this novel is that she wanted an own world. She presently lives in India with her parents and a sibling.